Rex Stout

REX STOUT, the creator of Nero Wolfe, was born in Nobles-
ville, Indiana, in 1886, the sixth of nine children of John and
Lucetta Todhunter Stout, both Quakers. Shortly after his
birth the family moved to Wakarusa, Kansas. He was educated in a country school, but by the age of nine he was
recognized throughout the state as a prodigy in arithmetic.
Mr. Stout briefly attended the University of Kansas but left
to enlist in the Navy and spent the next two years as a war-
rant officer on board President Theodore Roosevelt's yacht.
When he left the Navy in 1908, Rex Stout began to write
freelance articles and worked as a sight-seeing guide and
itinerant bookkeeper. Later he devised and implemented a
school banking system that was installed in four hundred
cities and towns throughout the country. In 1927 Mr. Stout
retired from the world of finance and, with the proceeds of
his banking scheme, left for Paris to write serious fiction. He
wrote three novels that received favorable reviews before
turning to detective fiction. His first Nero Wolfe novel, *Fer-
de-Lance*, appeared in 1934. It was followed by many others,
among them *Too Many Cooks*, *The Silent Speaker*, *If Death
Ever Slept*, *The Doorbell Rang*, and *Please Pass the Guilt*,
which established Nero Wolfe as a leading character on a
par with Erle Stanley Gardner's famous protagonist, Perry
Mason. During World War II Rex Stout waged a personal
campaign against Nazism as chairman of the War Writers'
Board, master of ceremonies of the radio program *Speaking
of Liberty*, and member of several national committees. After the war he turned his attention to mobilizing public opinion against the wartime use of thermonuclear devices, was
an active leader in the Authors Guild, and resumed writing
his Nero Wolfe novels. Rex Stout died in 1975 at the age of
eighty-eight. A month before his death he published his sev-
enty-second Nero Wolfe mystery, *A Family Affair*. Ten
years later a seventy-third Nero Wolfe mystery was discovered and published in *Death Times Three*.

The Rex Stout Library

REX STOUT

Bad for Business

BANTAM BOOKS

NEW YORK · TORONTO · LONDON · SYDNEY · AUCKLAND

A TECUMSEH FOX
MYSTERY

*This book is fiction. No resemblance is intended
between any character herein and any person,
living or dead; any such resemblance is
purely coincidental.*

BAD FOR BUSINESS

A Bantam Crime Line Book / published by arrangement
with the estate of the author

PUBLISHING HISTORY

Farrar & Rinehart edition published 1940
Bantam edition / June 1982
Bantam reissue edition / December 1995

ISBN 9780-553-76302-7

Published simultaneously in the United States and Canada

Bantam Books are published by Bantam Books, a division of Bantam Double-
day Dell Publishing Group, Inc. Its trademark, consisting of the words "Bantam Books" and the portrayal of a rooster, is Registered in U.S. Patent and
Trademark Office and in other countries. Marca Registrada. Bantam Books,
1540 Broadway, New York, New York 10036.

144915995

Bad for Business

Chapter 1

A my Duncan said to herself, aloud, in a tone of withering sarcasm, "Heaven protect the poor working girl! I'll go get me a job at the five and ten, something decent and domestic like the kitchenware counter. Wah!"

She squeezed the rinse water from the stockings she had been washing, hung them in a neat row along the shower-curtain rail, dried her hands, and left the bathroom to enter the modest little living room of the apartment on Grove Street which she shared with a friend. Facing south, it was often a cheerful little room with the sun slanting in through the two windows, but now the dim November gloom of an overcast day was no more cheerful than she was. As she picked up her watch from the table at one end of the sofa and fastened it to her wrist, she frowned at it. It said twelve o'clock, and since her lunch engagement at the Churchill with the man who either was or wasn't trying to blackmail Mrs. V. A. Grimsby was for one o'clock, and it would take only twenty minutes to get there, and she intended to be fifteen minutes late, there was nearly an hour ahead of her and nothing to do with it that she felt like doing.

She wandered into the bedroom and got her gray fur coat from the closet and made another start at the urgent problem of whether to spend eighty-three dollars having it remodeled. She certainly couldn't afford the eighty-three dollars, but just look at it, and anyway she should never have bought the thing, with her light brown hair and the faint coloring of her skin and her outlandish chartreuse eyes. Eighty-three dollars! She shrugged and said something, not complimentary, to the coat.

She returned to the living room and sat on the sofa with a magazine which she didn't open. As far as the lunch engagement with the blackmailer was concerned, it was not at all certain that she was going to keep it. She was faced with a problem even more urgent than the remodeling of the fur coat. She had taken the job, about a year ago, because (a) it had been offered to her, (b) it had sounded exciting, (c) the lawyer whose secretary she was had just proposed to her for the fifth time and it was getting scrummy, and (d) she was tired of writing ". . . this agreement, entered into this ——— day of January, 1939, by the Corrigan Construction Company, hereinafter called . . ." And now what? Well, it had certain aspects. There was something sneaky—but no, she would be honest, that wasn't it. The reason she felt the way she did about it was quite specific.

She wanted to quit. But she couldn't just quit, because there were things like rent and food and clothes to be considered. How did people save money, anyhow? There must be some kind of a trick to it. She got up to a hundred dollars in a savings bank once, but then that girl in the office had got into trouble, and poof it went, and how were you going to avoid things like that? Of course if you were a skunk—

The bell rang. With her mind still on her problem, she went to the kitchenette and pushed the button to release the latch of the vestibule door downstairs, and then came back to open the door from the living room to the outer hall. She stood on the threshold, hearing footsteps ascending the flight of stairs and supposing in an inactive corner of her mind that it would be laundry or something; but saw that it wasn't when a man in well-tailored brown reached her level and came at her along the poorly lit hall. Her fingers tightened around the doorknob they were grasping, but that could not be seen.

"For heaven's sake," she said, and felt that she should have cleared her throat before trying to speak.

"Good afternoon." The man took his hat off and faced her with a grin which might have been called sheepish but for the fact that all other evidence was against any such assumption. Though saved from being offensively handsome by a rather wide mouth and a nose too broad to be called noble, he was thoroughly presentable, and there was a comfortable, even faintly aggressive, assurance in the set of his shoulders and the action of all his muscles, walking and standing. Nevertheless, the grin could undeniably have been called sheepish.

She had cleared her throat and still had a tight grasp on the doorknob. "I suppose it is," she admitted. "I mean it's after noon. But I thought you were a big executive. Don't tell me you're peddling provisions and beverages from door to door."

"That's a nice dress," he said. "I could see it better in there where there's more light. I just want to—I won't keep you long."

"You certainly won't." She made room for him to pass within, shut the door, turned to him, and glanced at her watch. "I haven't time to show you any etchings, because I have to leave in about a minute to keep an engagement. And I'm sorry, but I don't need any beans or flour or canned peaches—"

"If I only have a minute," he cut her off, "I want to use it. What has happened?"

"Happened?" She smiled at him. "Well, Norway has taken the Germans off of the *City of Flint* and interned them, and President Roosevelt—"

"Please!" he begged. He wasn't grinning. "What are you trying to do, have some fun with me?"

"Good heavens, no." His eyes required to be met, and she met them, keeping, she hoped, an easy dancing smile in hers. "I wouldn't dream of trying to have fun with one of the ablest and shrewdest—"

"Oh, you wouldn't." He took a step toward her. "I don't know about my being able and shrewd, but I'm pretty well occupied during business hours. Do you think I'm in the habit of running off in the middle of the day to beg a girl to go to a football game?"

"Certainly not," she laughed. "You don't have to. You just snap your fingers, and scads of girls—"

"Excuse me. I came because it's—well, it's important to me. I mean you are. You phone and tell me casually that you can't have dinner with me tomorrow and you can't go to the game with me Saturday. You say things interfere but you won't say what things. You only stammer—"

"I didn't stammer!"

"Well, I don't mean stammer. I mean you didn't even bother to make up a plausible excuse. You just more or less give me to understand that all dates are off. And that doesn't make sense unless something has happened, because you certainly gave me the impression that you liked me and enjoyed being with me. Of course we've only been together five times in the three weeks since we met, and I don't mean necessarily that you liked me in the way I was beginning to like—I don't mean beginning either—I mean you know very well the kind of impression—for instance, I have never missed a Yale-Harvard game since I graduated twelve years ago, and I don't like to go to a football game with a girl, I like to go with men and always have until now—"

"I appreciated it deeply, Mr. Cliff, really I did—"

"You see? 'Mr. Cliff!' You were calling me Leonard. And now 'Mr. Cliff' with sarcasm, and you won't see me tomorrow and you won't go to the game Saturday and you won't say what has happened, and I have a right to expect—"

"Right?" Her brows went up. "Oh? Have you got rights?"

"Yes, I—but I don't—yes, I have!" His color was rising. "Now look—didn't you give me a reason to suppose—weren't we friends? Weren't we friends enough so that if you decide to go to a football game with me and then suddenly decide not to go, I have a right to ask you why? Tell me that!"

"I'm not going," said Amy firmly, with a frozen smile.

"Why not?"

She shook her head. "I just don't want to." She looked at her wrist, which was all right as a gesture, though she didn't see the time. "And really I mustn't be late—"

"You won't tell me?"

"There's nothing to tell." The smile cracked a little. "You seem to assume that if a girl decides she isn't going somewhere with you, something terrible must have happened. Don't you admit the possibility that she merely doesn't care to go?"

"Why, I—but you—" He was stuttering. He stopped abruptly, and stood staring at her, his color slowly deepening. After a moment her eyes dropped from his.

"I beg your pardon," he said stiffly. "I seem to have made some kind of mistake." He walked to the door and opened it, and was gone.

Amy stood, with no other movement than turning her head, until steps from the hall were no longer heard. Then she clattered into the bedroom, grabbed up the gray fur coat, threw it down again, sat on the edge of the bed, and stared at the top of the dressing table.

She muttered to herself, aloud, "I did a swell job of that, didn't I, though? And my voice is trembling. You admit your voice is trembling, do you, Miss Duncan? What, no tears? Supreme effort of the will, huh? He'll take a girl to the ball game, by golly, or he'll know the reason why. You'll fix your face, my fine girl, that's what you'll do, and you'll go to work, and you'll like it!"

She opened her compact.

At a few minutes before three that afternoon she emerged from the 54th Street entrance of the Churchill in the company of a slender smiling elegant middle-aged man, was handed by him into a taxi, and waved through the window at him as the taxi rolled away. The s.s.e.m. man was Mrs. Grimsby's blackmailer. The lunch with him had been barren of results, for she had been too much preoccupied with her own affairs to function effectively. Now, having made a decision, she was acting upon it without loss of time. She leaned forward and told the driver to go to the

59th Street station of the Ninth Avenue El. Since she regarded this excursion as private business and therefore the fare could not be put on her expense account, forty or fifty cents made a difference.

Leaving the El at 23rd Street, she walked three short blocks north and a long one west. The three-story brick building she stopped in front of was old and grimy-looking, with a cobbled driveway for trucks tunneled through its middle, and there was nothing there or at the pedestrian entrance to proclaim its status or reason for existence, but anyone tilting his head a little from across the street could have seen stretched along the expanse of the bricks of the upper story, enormous letters in dingy white paint:

TINGLEY'S TITBITS

Inside was a dingy hall and a dingy and dilapidated staircase, the deep hollows in the treads witnesses of thousands of impatient feet up and down through many patient years. On the floor above was a good deal of noise: the hum of machinery from behind wooden partitions to the ceiling, and, as Amy passed through a door in still another partition to the left, a clatter of typewriters and other sounds of a busy office. It was only an anteroom; more partitions confronted her; and through a window in one of them a gray-haired man peered out and told her in a cracked voice that he thought Mr. Tingley was somewhere in the building. Amy forgave his rheumy old eyes for not recognizing her, and was about to tell him her name when she heard it pronounced from another direction by a young man who had emerged from a nearby door, glanced at her, and altered his intended course to approach the window.

"Amy? Sure it is! Hello there!"

"Hello, Phil." She let his long bony fingers wrap themselves around the knuckles of her outstretched hand, and slanted her eyes up to the altitude of his bony face with its hollowed cheeks, hoping that her own face was not betraying the vague discomfort, the mild repulsion, she had always felt at the sight of him, especially his mouth with its hint of strain at the down-turning corners—the mouth, properly, of a fanatic or a fiend stoically enduring unheard of and ceaseless torture.

She smiled at him. "I haven't seen you for ages. How's technocracy?"

"Technocracy?" He frowned. "My God, I don't know. Somewhere on a junk heap, I guess."

"Oh." Amy was apologetic. "I thought it was the road to happiness or wealth. Or both."

"No, no. Never. It was perhaps a step in education. But truth, like life, is dynamic." He pulled a pamphlet from his pocket. "Here, read that. You'll have to read it several times to understand it . . ."

Amy took it and glanced at it. On its printed cover the most prominent word, in large black type, was WOMON. She looked up at him in astonishment.

"Woman?" she demanded. "Women? Phil! Don't tell me you've gone in for matriarchy! Or even—sex? My sex?"

"Of course not," he denied indignantly. "It has nothing to do with women or sex either. WOMON means WORK-MONEY. The basis of the world economic structure is money. The basis of money is—has been—gold. It is antiquated and unsound, it no longer functions. What does a dollar of our currency represent? A speck of gold. Ridiculous! It has been proposed to base the dollar on commodities instead of gold. On potatoes and wool and iron! Even more ridiculous! Commodities are even more unstable than gold. The basis of money must be stable, solid, unalterable. What is stable? What is the most stable thing in the world?"

He tapped her on the shoulder with a forefinger. "The work of a man! That's stable!" He stretched out his arms. "What these hands can do!" He tapped his temple. "What this head can do! That's the basis, the only sound basis, for the world's money! Work-Money! We call it Womon!"

"I see," Amy nodded. "It sounds sensible, but I still think it looks and sounds too much like woman. You'll have trouble with that, see if you don't." She stuffed the pamphlet into her bag. "I'll read this over. I don't know about several times, but I'll read it. Is Uncle Arthur in his office?"

"Yes. I just left him. I'd be glad to send you a bunch of those, if you'd care to pass them around."

"I'd better read it first. I might not like it." Amy offered a hand. "Nice to see you again. Hooray for happiness and wealth."

That was indiscreet, for it started him on Womon's explanation of the true nature of wealth, but after a few minutes she succeeded in heading him off. Soon after he had gone, through a door that led toward the hum of machinery, word came for her to penetrate to Mr. Tingley's office. To get there she had to pass through two or three more partitions, exchange greetings with women and girls at desks who called her Amy, and traverse a long wide passageway. As she stopped at a door on the frosted glass panel of which THOMAS TINGLEY was inscribed, her shoulders moved with a little shiver of discomposure. She had forgotten about that. There was no Thomas Tingley and had not been for all of her twenty-five years and then some. It was his grandson she was calling on. To keep his name painted there on the door had always struck her—she shrugged the shiver off, and entered.

Though Thomas Tingley no longer occupied that room, certainly his office furniture did. The old-fashioned roll-top desk was battered and scarred, the varnish on the chair seats had long since been rubbed away, and the ancient massive safe was anything but streamlined. Wherever shelves and cabinets left enough wall space for a large framed photograph, one was there, the oldest and most faded, of a hundred or more men and women in strange and ludicrous costumes, bearing the hand-printed legend: *Tingley's Titbits Employees Picnic, Colton Beach, Long Island, July 4th, 1891.* A large folding screen of green burlap, at Amy's right as she entered, concealed, as she knew, a marble wash basin with hot and cold running water which, say what you please about it, had once been so de luxe as to be next door to sybaritic.

She knew all three of the people whose conversation her entrance had interrupted. The plump fussy-looking man at the desk, with hair not really gray but showing signs of it, was Arthur Tingley, grandson of the name on the door. The one with hair completely gray, even white, standing like a parson with his hands behind his back and four buttons on his coat, all buttoned, was Sol Fry, the sales manager. The woman, somewhere between the two men as to age, who in case of need could have been transformed instantly into the commanding officer of a Women's Battalion by merely buying her a uniform, was G. Yates, devoid of title in the unincorporated firm, but actually in charge of production. No one was supposed to know that the G. stood for Gwendolyn; Amy had learned it inadvertently from Phil Tingley.

They greeted her, Sol Fry and G. Yates amicably enough though without exuberance, Arthur Tingley with a frown of irritation and a voice to match. The greetings over, he demanded brusquely:

"I suppose that Bonner woman sent you here? Have you accomplished anything?"

Amy counted three, as she had decided to do, knowing in advance that this interview would require self-control in the face of provocation. "I'm afraid," she said calmly and, she hoped, not aggressively, "we haven't accomplished much. But Miss Bonner didn't send me. I came personally—I mean not officially— not from Miss Bonner. There's something I think I ought to tell you." She glanced at the other two. "Privately."

"What do you mean?" He was glancing at her. "Do you mean a private matter? What kind of a private matter? This is a business firm and these are business hours!"

"We'll go," said G. Yates in a decided but surprisingly soprano voice. "Come on, Sol—"

"No!" Tingley snapped. "You stay."

But the woman had Sol Fry's elbow and was steering him to a door; not the one Amy had entered by. As she opened it she turned:

"She's your niece and she wants to talk with you. We ought to be taking a look anyhow."

The closing door rattled the partition. Tingley frowned at it, then at his niece, and snapped. "Well? Now that you've interrupted an important conference to bother me with your private affairs—"

"I didn't say it was my private affair. I didn't know

I was interrupting a conference. I was told to come on in."

"Certainly you were! I wanted to tell you something! I wanted to tell you that I learned only this morning that it was you who had been put to work on this thing, and I told that Bonner woman that I didn't trust you and I wouldn't have it!" Tingley slapped the desk with his palm. "And I won't! If she has already told you and that's what you came to see me about, I'll give you three minutes by my watch!" He pulled it from his vest pocket.

Amy felt that she was trembling, and knew that she was beyond the point where counting three would help any. He was simply too impossible. But though she had failed to control her adrenaline, she would at all events control her voice, and she succeeded. "You may be my mother's brother," she said firmly and clearly, "but you're a troglodyte," and turned and left the room, paying no attention to the sputtering behind her.

She retraced her way through the labyrinth of partitions, on through the anteroom, to the head of the creaky old stairs, and descended to the street, and walked east at a brisk and determined pace. She was good and mad. So the miserable creature had told Miss Bonner he didn't trust her, had he? But that was nothing worse than a minor irritation, since she had explained things to Miss Bonner when the assignment had been given her. She considered that for a block, and passed on to other aspects. At Seventh Avenue she turned south and, getting warm, unfastened the gray fur coat to let in some air.

If she lost her job, that would be bad. She had to have a job, and this was a pretty good one. But it was a very complicated and confused situation. Very. In spite of that, she had decided what to do, and had gone to do it, and had failed because she had got mad at Uncle Arthur when he had acted as she had known he would act. Now it was just as complicated and confused as ever.

Preoccupied, buried in her problem, she bumped into people twice, which wasn't like her. At Fourteenth Street she did something more perilous. Stepping down from the curb and emerging incautiously from behind a parked taxi, she walked smack into the bumper of a passing car and was knocked flat.

Chapter 2

Hands helped her to her feet and supported her. Though she was not ordinarily testy, she was unreasonably irritated at being supported by strange hands, and shook herself loose; and nearly fell again from dizziness. Voices asked if she was hurt, and she made a vaguely negative reply. A cop came trotting up, grasped her arm firmly, and escorted her to the sidewalk.

Her head cleared enough for her to realize that she was filled with rage. She told the cop in a quavering voice, "Please let go of me. I'm not hurt. I walked right into it. Let me—"

"Wait a minute," put in a voice not the cop's. "My car hit you. Look at you, you're covered with dirt. You don't know whether you're hurt or not. I'll drive you to a doctor."

"I don't need a doctor." Amy, still a little dizzy, raised her head and was looking into a face with brown eyes, a nose and chin not quite pointed, and a mouth that smiled at the corners. It was the compelling and convincing quality of the eyes, focused at hers, though she didn't stop to consider it, that led her to add immediately, "But you can drive me home—if you—it isn't very far—"

The cop put in, "I'd better look at your license."

The man produced it. The cop took it and read the name, and looked up with a grin of surprised interest. "Oh, yeah? Pleased to meetcha." He handed it back. Amy took the man's proffered arm, found in three steps that she didn't need it, and permitted herself to be assisted into the front seat of a dark-blue Wethersill convertible. Her right knee hurt a little and she wanted to look at it, but decided to wait. There was another man in the back seat. As the car rolled forward the man beside her asked:

"Up or down?"

"Down, please. 320 Grove Street."

After the car circled south into the clutter of traffic on Seventh Avenue nothing was said for three blocks, when the man driving spoke abruptly, keeping his eyes straight ahead:

"Your fingers are short."

"Not only that," came from the back seat, in a baritone with a strong foreign accent that sounded deliberately musical, "but her eyes are the color that they painted the front bathroom upstairs."

"Excuse me," said the driver. "That's Mr. Pokorny back there. Miss—"

"Duncan," said Amy, feeling too shaken to twist her head for confirmation of her acquaintance with Mr. Pokorny. "He seems to be whimsical. As far as that's concerned, so do you. I regret my fingers being too short, but I'm perfectly satisfied—"

"I said short, not too short. It was meant as a compliment. I don't like women who look as if their fingers and legs and necks had undergone a stretching process."

"Everyone in America," said the back seat, "regards Russians as whimsical."

Amy tried turning her head. It gave her a twinge in the left shoulder, but she made it far enough to see a round innocent face whose owner might have been anything between thirty and fifty, with baby-blue wide-open eyes. One of the eyes winked at her with an indescribably cheerful carnality, and she winked back without meaning to.

She faced around to look at the driver and inquired, "And your name?"

"Fox."

"Fox?"

"Fox."

"Oh." She regarded his profile, and saw that from the side his nose looked more pointed and his chin less. "That might account for the cop's being pleased to meet you. I'd better look at your license."

Without glancing aside, he got the little leather folder from his pocket and handed it to her. She opened it and saw the name neatly printed in accordance with instructions: TECUMSEH FOX.

"The sword of justice and the scourge of crime," said Pokorny. "Do you know who he is?"

"Certainly." Amy returned the license. "I would anyway, only it happens that I'm a detective too, though of course infinitely obscure compared to him."

"Now who's being whimsical?" Fox demanded.

"Not me. Really. I'm an operative for a private agency. I may not be tomorrow, but I am today—it's farther down, there just the other side of the awning—"

The car rolled to a stop at the curb in front of Number 320, and Pokorny emerged from the back and opened the front door on her side.

"I'm glad no bones were broken," said Fox.

"So am I." Amy didn't move. "I walked right into you. If I felt like laughing, that would be especially funny."

"Why?"

"Oh—" She fluttered a hand. "Reasons. You were very nice not to run over me." She looked at him, full face now, hesitated, and then went on. "I've just made a decision. I'm not usually so impulsive—" She stopped.

"Go ahead."

"But I'm in a jam, and if by pure luck I find myself on speaking terms with Tecumseh Fox—of course I don't know whether detectives exchange professional courtesies the way doctors do—you know a doctor never charges another doctor for treatment or advice —and you have a reputation for a heart as warm as your head is cool—"

"And your fingers are short," said Pokorny from the sidewalk.

Fox was frowning at her. "Which do you need, treatment or advice?"

"Advice. I'll make it as brief as I can—but there's no use sitting out here in the cold—"

"All right, climb out." Fox followed her to the sidewalk, and turned to Pokorny: "There's a drugstore at the corner. Would you mind phoning Stratton we'll be late and waiting here in the car?"

"I would," Pokorny declared. "I'm fairly cold myself."

"Then you can wait in the drugstore and drink chocolate. If you heard Miss Duncan's story you'd base a new theory of human conduct on it, and you have too many already."

Pokorny took it with a cheerful nod and another

wink at Amy, and they left him. She limped a little, but declined assistance mounting the stairs. In the living room of her apartment, Fox insisted that she should first go and take a look at herself, so she hobbled to the bedroom and made enough of an examination to establish that except for soiled clothing, ruined stockings, and a bruised knee, the damage was slight. Then she returned and sat on the sofa with him on a chair facing her, and told him:

"The chief trouble is: I think I have to quit my job, and I can't afford to and don't want to."

"Who do you work for?"

"Bonner & Raffray. They have an office on Madison Avenue—"

Fox nodded. "I know. Run by Dol Bonner. Based on the fact that most men get careless sooner or later when they're talking to a pretty woman, especially if the woman is also clever and can guide a conversation. But I should think your eyes would put a man on guard."

"What's wrong with my eyes?"

"Nothing. They're very interesting. Excuse me. Go ahead."

"Well, I've been working there about a year. I lived in Nebraska with my parents, and five years ago, when I was twenty, my mother died, and soon afterwards I came to New York and my uncle gave me a job in his office. I didn't like it much, mostly on account of my uncle, but I stayed nearly a year and then left and got a job in a law office."

"If your incompatibility with your uncle is important, tell me about it."

"I don't know that it's important, but it has a bearing—that's why I mentioned it. He's ill-mannered and quick-tempered and generally disagreeable, but the quarrel—what brought it to a head was his attitude about unmarried mothers."

"Oh." Fox nodded.

"Oh, no." Amy shook her head. "Not me. It was a girl who worked in the canning department, but I learned that it had happened twice before in previous years. He simply fired her, and you should have heard him. I got mad and told him what I thought of him, and quit before he could fire me too. I had been working in the law office for three years, and was the secretary of a member of the firm, when I met Miss Bonner and she offered me a job and I took it. Do you know her?"

"Never met her."

"Well—talk about clever women." Amy, without thinking, started to cross her knees, grimaced, and forbore. "You ought to hear her coaching me on a job. I'm the youngest of the four women on what she calls her siren squad. When I'm on a case I'm not allowed to go to the office and if I meet her accidentally I'm not supposed to speak to her. Last spring I got evidence for—but I guess I shouldn't tell you that."

"Are you on a case now?"

"Yes. Have you ever heard of Tingley's Titbits?"

"Certainly. Appetizers in glass jars with a red label showing a goat eating a peacock's tail. Lots of different varieties. Expensive but good."

"They're better than good, they're the best you can buy. I admit that. But a month ago they began to have quinine in them."

Fox cocked a surprised eye at her. "I beg your pardon?"

"Yes, they did. Complaints began to come in that they tasted bitter, couldn't be eaten, and thousands of jars were returned by dealers, and when they were

analyzed some of them were found to contain quanti-
ties of quinine. Tingley—Mr. Arthur Tingley, the
present head of the firm—engaged Dol Bonner to investigate."

"Do you know how he happened to pick Miss Bonner?"

Amy nodded. "For quite a while P. & B. has been
trying to buy the Tingley business—"

"Do you mean the Provisions & Beverages Corporation?"

"That's it. The food octopus. They offered three
hundred thousand dollars for the business. One of
their vice-presidents has been working on it quite a
while, but Tingley refused to sell. He said the name
alone, with the prestige it has established over seventy years, was worth half a million. So when this
trouble occurred, the only thing they could think of
was that P. & B. had bribed someone in the factory to
put in the quinine, to give Tingley such a headache
that he would be glad to sell and get out. They started
their own investigation among the employees, but
they thought something might be done from the other
end."

"And they set Bonner on the P. & B."

"Yes. A woman named Yates is in charge of production at the Tingley factory, which is up on Twenty-
sixth Street. She knew of Miss Bonner because they
are both members of the Manhattan Business
Women's League. At her suggestion Tingley engaged
Dol Bonner, and I was assigned to work on the
P. & B. vice-president who had been trying to make a
deal with Tingley. I told Miss Bonner that Arthur
Tingley was my uncle and that I had once worked for
him, and had quarreled with him and quit, but she

said that shouldn't disqualify me for the job and the rest of the squad were busy."

"Was it agreeable to Tingley?"

"He didn't know about it. I hadn't seen him for a long time, and he didn't even know I was working for Bonner & Raffray. At least I don't suppose he did. But he told me this afternoon that he had learned this morning that I was working on his case, and he had told Miss Bonner that he didn't trust me and he wouldn't have it."

"And you're afraid you'll lose your job and that's the jam you're in."

Amy shook her head. "That's not it. Or only a small part of it. I got acquainted with—uh—the P. & B. vice-president three weeks ago, and started—that is, I proceeded with the investigation. He's young and quite presentable, competent and assured and rather—I imagine pretty aggressive as a business man. We got—on fairly good terms. Then, Saturday afternoon, I saw him in a booth at Rusterman's Bar, having what appeared to be a very confidential conversation with Dol Bonner."

"The poor devil," Fox laughed. "With two of you after him—"

"Oh, no," Amy protested. "That's the trouble. If she had been working him, she would certainly have let me know. I was given to understand that she had never met him or even seen him. This morning, when I phoned her, I gave her an opening to tell me about her meeting with him Saturday, but she still pretended she had never seen him. So obviously she is double-crossing Tingley. And making a fool of me."

Fox frowned and pursed his lips. "Not obviously. Conceivably."

"Obviously," Amy insisted stubbornly. "I've tried

to think of another explanation, and there isn't any. You should have seen how confidential they were."

"They didn't see you?"

"No. I've been trying to decide what to do. Much as I dislike my uncle, I can't just go ahead with it as if I thought it was on the square. Miss Bonner pays me, but the money comes from Tingley's Titbits, and while I may not be a saint I hope I have my share of plain ordinary honesty. Just after I phoned her this morning, before I stopped to think I called up—the vice-president and canceled two dates I had with him. That was silly, because it didn't really settle anything. Then I—excuse me—"

The telephone was ringing. She went to it, at a corner of the table, and spoke:

"Hello . . . Oh, hello . . . No, I haven't . . . No, really . . . I'm sorry, but I can't help it if you misunderstood. . . ."

After several more phrases, equally unrevealing, she hung up and returned to her chair. Incautiously she met Fox's gaze, and again the compelling expectancy in his eyes caused her to speak without meaning to.

"That was the P. & B. vice-president," she said.

Fox smiled at her and inquired pleasantly. "About the canceled dates? By the way, what's wrong with his name?"

"Nothing that I know of."

"I just wondered. You keep calling him the vice-president, but surely you know his name, don't you?"

"Certainly. Leonard Cliff."

"Thanks. You were saying . . ."

"I was going to say that I went to see my uncle."

"Today?"

"Yes, right after lunch. I hated to lose my job, and

I decided to tell him the facts and try to persuade him to take the case away from Bonner & Raffray without giving a reason, and turn it over to some other agency. I was going to offer to return to him my pay for the three weeks I had been working on it. It seemed to me that was a fair thing to do. But the minute he saw me he began yelling about how he had told Miss Bonner he didn't trust me and didn't want me working on it, and if I had told him what I intended to he would instantly have phoned Miss Bonner about it, which I might have known anyhow if I had used my head. So I got mad and called him an ape, only I said troglodyte, and left."

She stopped. Fox prodded her, "Go ahead."

"That's all. I started to walk home, and before I got here I walked into your car."

"But you said you're in a jam."

Amy stared. "Well, good heavens, aren't I?"

"Not that I can see. Unless you've left something out."

"Then you must have an exalted idea of a jam," Amy declared indignantly. "The least that can happen is that I lose my job. That may seem very picayune to you, with your ten-thousand-dollar fees, but it's darned important to me. And anyway, if I just quit and let it go at that, how about the double-cross they're putting over on my uncle? I may dislike him, in fact I do, but that's all the more reason why I don't want to have a hand in a game to cheat him."

"You won't have a hand in it if you quit your job."

"But I don't want to quit!"

"I suppose not. And that's all? That's the jam you're in?"

"Yes."

Fox regarded her a moment, and said quietly, "I think you're lying."

She stared, gulped, and demanded, "I'm lying?"

"I think so."

Her eyes flashed. "Oh, well," she said, and rose to her feet.

"Now wait a minute." Fox, otherwise not moving, was smiling up at her. "You've asked for some professional courtesy, so you're going to get it. You may not know you're lying, or let's say misrepresenting; it may be only that something is interfering with your mental processes. Some uncontrollable emotion. There are two things wrong with your story. First, your unwarranted assumption that because you saw Miss Bonner talking with the vice-president—there, I caught it from you—she is double-crossing Tingley. There are any number of possible explanations besides that. Second, the obvious thing to do is to tell Miss Bonner that by accident you saw her with Leonard Cliff. Just tell her that, of course without any intimation that you suspect her of skulduggery. She may give an explanation that will completely relieve your conscience. If she doesn't, you can then decide what to do. Don't tell me that anyone with eyes as intelligent as yours hasn't thought of as obvious a step as that."

"But I was scared to. I was too afraid of losing my job to do anything—"

"Oh, no, you weren't. You did do something drastic. You canceled two dates with Mr. Cliff. What for? In case there was an innocent reason for the Bonner-Cliff conversation, those dates were an important function of the job you don't want to lose. You were too befuddled to think straight. Befuddled by what? Well, you canceled the dates with Cliff in a fit of pique. When you were describing him to me you faltered and broke a sentence off in the middle. You didn't want to pronounce his name, and when you did pronounce it because I asked for it, your voice changed. When you talked to him on the phone just now, you turned your back on me, but not enough so that I couldn't see the color in your cheek. You're in a jam, I admit that, but in the last twenty centuries there have been billions of girls in the kind of jam you're in. You have acquired a tender sentiment for Mr. Cliff. Is he married?"

Amy said, in a small voice, "No." She sat down and looked at Fox's dark-red necktie, and after a moment lifted her gaze to meet his eyes. "I deny it," she said aggressively.

"Why? Why deny it?"

"Because it isn't true."

Fox shrugged. "You tricked me," he declared. "What you need isn't Tecumseh Fox, it's Dorothy Dix. I suppose what irks you most is that you were nursing a belief that the P. & B. vice-president was inclined to reciprocate in the matter of sentiment, but if he is secretly in cahoots with Miss Bonner he must know that you are merely doing professional work on him and therefore his own apparent reactions are open to suspicion. Of course on that point I can't help you any, but I should think your feminine intuition—"

Amy jumped up and made for the bedroom, not hobbling, and from the inside closed the door.

Fox sat for five seconds, looking at the door, raised brows widening his eyes. Then he sighed, arose, got his hat from the table, and started for the entrance to the hall. Halfway there he stopped abruptly, wheeled, sailed his hat through the air to an accurate landing in the center of the table, went to the bedroom door and opened it, and entered.

"About the advice you asked for," he said

brusquely. "I think you ought to go ahead and tell Bonner you saw her with Cliff, and also tell her that you have become infected with a personal attitude toward him which disqualifies you for this assignment. That way you may keep your job."

"I am not infected!" said Amy hotly. She stood facing him. "And I assure you I don't care—his reactions—what do I care whether—"

"There's a bell ringing."

"I can hear it, thank you."

Fox moved aside to give her free passage to the door, which was standing open. She disappeared from his line of vision, but he heard a pause in her footsteps, a sound which he detected as the punching of a latch button, and her footsteps again; and as he saw her recrossing the living room he called, "Do you want me out of here?"

Amy replied curtly, "Do as you please," and continued to the door to the hall, which she opened. On the threshold she stood bracing herself, arranging her muscles and preparing her face obviously not in expectation of the laundry boy; but if by any chance what she did expect was the P. & B. vice-president, her preparation for the encounter was in vain. A woman ascended the stairs to her view and came down the hall—a woman of thirty, smart and compact in a handsome tweed suit and a conventionally perky hat, with yellow-brown alert eyes in a rather narrow but attractive face.

"Oh," said Amy in a voice unnecessarily loud. "Good afternoon, Miss Bonner."

"Hello, Amy."

She entered as Amy made gangway, and circled the room with a glance as Amy closed the door.

"Sit on the sofa," Amy invited her. "As you have discovered, it's the only comfortable seat we have."

"Thanks," Miss Bonner, standing, indicated with a nod the hat in the center of the table. "Is there someone here?"

"Why—oh, the hat." A swift glance had already told Amy that the bedroom door had been closed, all but a crack. She tried a little bubble of a laugh and it came out very well. "No, that's just a souvenir."

"Instead of a scalp?" Miss Bonner smiled, not warmly, but nevertheless it was a smile. "Not Mr. Dickinson? Or is it?"

"Oh, no, I haven't got very far with him."

"I suppose not. He's probably wary." Miss Bonner sat on the sofa. "I only have a minute. I had to go downtown and stopped in. You didn't phone at three o'clock to report."

"No, I—I'm sorry." Amy sat on the chair. "I didn't leave Mr. Dickinson until after three, and then I had an errand, and I thought I'd wait till I got home to phone—and on the way here, if you'll believe it, I actually walked into a car and got knocked down, and that shook me up—"

"Did you get hurt?"

"Nothing to speak of. Only a bruised knee."

"I like to receive reports on schedule, Amy."

"Of course you do. I'm sorry. This is my first offense, Miss Bonner."

"I know it is. So I'll overlook it. I'm taking you off of the Tingley case."

"Oh?" Amy gawked at her. "Taking me—" She stopped.

"Yes. Your uncle phoned this morning and raised cain. Unluckily, his son—it seems he has a son—"

Amy nodded. "My cousin Phil."

"Well, his son saw you at the theater the other evening with Mr. Cliff, and told him about it this morning, and when he phoned me and asked a question I had to answer it. He said he didn't trust you and spoke slightingly of your moral standards, and so forth, and said he didn't want you connected with his affairs." Miss Bonner upturned her palms. "So that's that, my dear. I must say, in view of your uncle's manners, I'm not surprised you didn't get along with him. For the present you can concentrate on Mr. Dickinson. Did you make any progress today?"

"Nothing worth mentioning. He's pretty hard to handle." Amy shifted in her chair. "But I—about the Tingley case—I'm glad you're taking me off. So that's all right—but there's something I wanted to tell you —not that I have any reason to suppose it was connected with the Tingley case, actually—but I just thought I should tell you that I saw you at Rusterman's Bar Saturday with Mr. Cliff."

Miss Bonner's alert eyes narrowed slightly. "You did?"

Amy nodded. "I was there with Mr. Dickinson, and I saw you—not that it has any significance, of course, but—"

"But what?"

"I thought I ought to tell you."

"Why?"

"Well—I had understood you to say that you didn't know Mr. Cliff and had never seen him, and I thought—one thing I thought was that perhaps you didn't know it was him, and I should tell you—"

"I see," said Miss Bonner, with ice suddenly in her voice. "I wondered what you were trying to get at on the phone this morning. Thank you for making it clear. You were trying to find out if I knew who I was

associating with, so that if I didn't you could tell me."
The ice in her voice got colder. "Since you thought
you ought to tell me, why didn't you do so?"

"You mean this morning," Amy muttered.

"I mean this morning."

"Well, I—I *am* telling you—"

"You're floundering," Miss Bonner gestured impatiently. "I told you, Amy, when I hired you, that the
first requisite in the detective business is completely
unadulterated trustworthiness. Most of the things a
detective does are necessarily secret and confidential,
and an operative whose reliability is in any degree
open to suspicion is no longer of any value. I don't
know what you're hiding from me, but you're hiding
something. I don't like it. I don't like it a bit." She
suddenly and energetically arose and pointed at the
middle of the table. "And another thing I don't like is
that hat. Souvenir? Souvenir of what?"

She moved with such unexpected swiftness that
Amy merely sat and goggled at her, helpless. Darting
to the bedroom door, with a hand extended to push it
open, Miss Bonner stopped as abruptly as she had
started, when it swung wide just before she reached
it and her path was blocked by the solid figure of a
man who stood there smiling at her. She fell back a
step.

"Flagrante," he said. "There's no doubt of that,
but not delicto. How do you do, Miss Bonner. I've
heard of you."

She regarded him from head to foot, and back up
again, and then turned her back on him without returning the amenity. She spoke to the youngest member of her siren squad, and the ice had become dry ice:

"Apparently your uncle knows what he's talking
about. I'll mail you a check for last week. I'll hold up

the release on your bond until I find out whether you've forfeited it or not."

"But Miss Bonner!" Amy was pleading. "There's nothing wrong—if you'll let me—"

"Bosh. I find a rival—but no, I won't flatter myself that Tecumseh Fox would consider himself a rival of Dol Bonner—I find an eminent detective in your apartment, and that alone is enough, without adding that he is concealed in your bedroom while I am discussing my business with you—" She broke off, turned, and smiled sarcastically at the man. "But why do I go on talking, Mr. Fox? Silly, isn't it?"

"Fatuous," Fox agreed, returning the smile. "It's because you're mad." He moved past her, toward the door to the hall. "You'd better walk it off." He opened the door and politely held it for her. Without another glance at her ex-employee, she walked to it, and passed through, and he closed the door behind her.

"You might—" Amy stopped to get better control of her voice. Her chin worked, and then she began again, "You might have helped me—you might—instead of shoving her out—"

Fox shook his head. "Not a chance. I couldn't deny I'm a detective, and how was I going to explain being here? If I had said my car hit you and I brought you home, I would only have made myself ridiculous. You know that. It's one of the oldest gags in the business, especially with female operatives. I wouldn't be surprised if that was the way you introduced yourself to Mr. Leonard Cliff. Wasn't it?"

Amy stood staring at him, biting her lip, breathing visibly.

"Wasn't it?"

She nodded.

"So," Fox nodded back, "it would have gone over

big if I had tried to dish that out for her. I did have a tale ready that would probably have done the trick, but I couldn't trust you for your end. You're all in pieces. I can't blame you much, since in Mr. Cliff you seem to have picked on one who puts quinine in people's food and hoodwinks you by consorting with your boss—"

"He didn't—I didn't—"

"Consort means merely to associate."

Amy threw herself onto the sofa and buried her face in a cushion.

Fox stood frowning down at her. After a little he turned and strode toward the open doorway to the kitchenette, and in five paces swiftly pivoted his head to the rear; but if he expected to find her peeking he was disappointed. All he did in the kitchenette was drink two glasses of water from the faucet, letting it run a while first; then he returned to the sofa and saw that her shoulders were still making little jerks.

He spoke to the back of her head. "I'm late for an appointment, Miss Duncan, and I have to go. Your difficulties are pretty complicated. I'm in a slight one myself, because the minute I saw your eyes I fell in love with you, but we can ignore that because I'm doing it all the time. Are you listening?"

Her "yes" was muffled, but it got to him.

"Well. Your personal involvement with Mr. Cliff is out of my line, and anyway I am temporarily his rival for your affections. Did you hear the temporarily?"

"Yes."

"Okay. As for your job, that depends on how good an operative you are. If you're good, we can probably smooth it over with Miss Bonner after she cools off. We can't possibly tell her you walked into my car, but I can sound extremely plausible if my heart's in it, and for the present my heart is yours. However, the real point is that I was born curious. I can't explain why I have a feeling that whoever put quinine in Tingley's Titbits was daring me to find it out and prove it, but I have. I used to pretend I could ignore such things, but I can't. So I'm not going to."

He got his hat from the table. "You'll hear from me. I don't know when. I'm in the Westchester phone book. So long."

Chapter 3

A
t eleven o'clock the following morning, Tuesday, there were three persons in the dingy anteroom of the Tingley offices on the second floor of the old building on 26th Street: a red-faced youth getting his change and a receipted bill at the cashier's window, a man in a gray suit waiting on a chair, and another man on another chair looking ferociously patient, with a large sample case on the floor between his feet. The seated men watched the youth pocket his change and leave. Soon afterward a door leading within opened and a man emerged—an erect man of sixty in a conservative and expensive topcoat and dark felt hat to match—and left by the exit to the hall. His appearance seemed to remind the man in the gray suit of something, for he got out a notebook and pencil, wrote in a neat hand, "GJ88 at TT Tues.," and returned the tools to his pocket.

Five minutes later noises issued from the aperture of the cashier's window. The man in the gray suit, deducing that they were intended for him, arose and approached. The old man with rheumy eyes peered through and said:

"Mr. Tingley is very busy. He wants to know what you want to see him about."

The man in the gray suit got out the tools again, tore out a sheet from the notebook and wrote on it, "Quinine," folded it and handed it through the hole.

"Send that to him, please."

In another three minutes he was invited inside and a woman with a snub nose appeared to conduct him to the room whose door still said THOMAS TINGLEY. He entered, said good morning politely, and told the man seated at the roll-top desk that it was Mr. Arthur Tingley he had asked to see.

"I'm Arthur Tingley." The plump but sagging face of the man at the desk looked as harried and exasperated as his voice sounded. He exhibited a slip of paper. "What the devil is this? Who are you?"

"I sent my name in. Fox. A man by the name of Fox." The visitor pre-empted a chair that was by the corner of the desk, and smiled pleasantly. "I live up in the country, up near Brewster. Last week I bought some jars of Tingley's Titbits, and when one of them was opened it tasted bitter. A chemist friend of mine analyzed it for me, and he says it has quinine in it. How do you suppose that happened?"

"I don't know," said Tingley shortly. "Where is it?"

"The jar? My friend still has it."

"What kind was it?"

"Liver Pâté Number Three."

Tingley grunted. "Where did you buy it?"

"At Bruegel's on Madison Avenue."

"Bruegel's? My God! That's the first—" Tingley stopped abruptly and regarded his caller with a flinty stare.

"I rather supposed," said Fox sympathetically,

"that I was bringing you some startling news, but apparently not. You see, I'm a detective. Tecumseh Fox. You may possibly have heard of me."

"How the devil would I hear of you?"

"I thought you might be one of the few who have." Only the perceptive eyes of a Pokorny would have caught the faint flicker of his vanity's discomfiture. "No matter. The point is that, being trained to observe, I remark that your lack of astonishment and the sentence you chopped off indicate that you've heard of quinine before. Do you know how it got into your liver pâté?"

"No. I don't." Tingley wriggled in his chair. "I realize, Mr. Fox, that you certainly have a justifiable complaint—"

"I'm not complaining." Fox waved the idea away. "Why, have you had a lot of complaints?"

"We . . . there have been a few . . ."

"Any from the pure food people? The government? Or have any of the newspapers—"

"My God, no! There's no reason—there's nothing dangerous about quinine—"

"That's true. But it isn't much of an appetizer, and it isn't on the label. As I say, though, I am not complaining. What I'm really here for is to call to your attention the damage someone might do, me for instance, by informing the government or sicking a newspaper like the *Gazette* on it. Or both. Not that I'm going to do it. I'm merely threatening to do it."

Tingley leaned forward and surveyed his caller with an angry glare. Fox smiled at him. Finally Tingley said in a strained voice, "You are, are you?"

"I am."

"Why, you—" Tingley was trembling with rage. "You dirty scoundrel—" His jaw continued to move, but for a moment there were no more words. Then he managed some: "By God, you'll tell *me* something! Who are you working for? The P. & B.?" He spat the hated initials from him.

"I'm working for no one but myself—"

"Like hell you are! So this is the squeeze, is it?" Tingley thrust out a trembling fist. "You can tell Mr. Cliff—"

"You're wrong. I don't know any Mr. Cliff. This is my own private personal idea. I thought it up alone."

Fox's tone could carry conviction when required, and it did then. Tingley sat back and scowled at him with his lips compressed to a thin line. At length he growled:

"Private personal blackmail. Huh?"

"That's right."

"What do you want?"

"I want to inspect your factory and talk with your employees. I want to do whatever is necessary to find out who put quinine in that stuff. I'm an investigator and I want to investigate."

"Of course you do." Tingley was savagely sarcastic. "And how much am I to pay you for it?"

"Nothing. Not a cent. It's none of your business why I want to do it, since you'll be permitting it under duress anyway, so we'll just say I want to satisfy my curiosity. The fact is, you're getting a break. I am a good detective. Do you know any police officials? You must, since you've been in business here all your life. Call up one of them and ask about me." Fox reached in his pocket for the leather fold containing his driving license, opened it and handed it across. "There's the name."

Tingley looked at it, grunted something, hesitated, and reached for his phone. After getting a number he asked for Captain Darst, and in a moment started asking questions. He covered the ground thoroughly, even to the point of reciting a detailed description of Fox's appearance, and finally hung up and swiveled to face the caller again.

He looked a little relieved, but not satisfied. "Who sent you?" he demanded.

"No one," said Fox patiently. "Don't start that again. You must be pretty busy. Just give me a passport to the premises and forget about me."

"You must be some kind of a damn fool."

"Certainly I am. Right now I ought to be up home helping with a dormant sulfur spray on my peach trees, and look what I'm doing. Look at you. You ought to be out on the road trotting five miles under wraps, but here you are."

"Are you from Consolidated Cereals?"

"I am not from anybody."

"Exactly what do you want to do?"

"What I said. Look your factory over and ask questions of people. You can hitch a trusted subordinate to my elbow."

"You're damned right I can. You're either a liar or you're crazy. In either case—" Tingley reached for a row of old-fashioned massive bell pushes and pressed his finger on the second from the left. Then he leaned back and glowered at the other in silence during the moments that lapsed before a door in the side wall opened. A woman appeared—a woman over fifty but probably not sixty, with a figure of generous proportions, a muscular face and efficient-looking dark eyes—and approached them with energetic steps.

"We're just starting some mixes on the middle run—"

"I know," Tingley cut her off. "Just a minute, Miss

Yates. This man's name is Fox. He's a detective. He's going to look around the factory, and he can ask questions of you or Sol or Carrie or Edna or Thorpe. No one else. I don't trust him. I'll explain later why he's here. One of you stay with him."

"Does he go in the sauce room?"

"Yes, but hold up while he's there."

Miss Yates, obviously too busy to waste time on questions, nodded at Fox and said crisply, "Come on."

When he was alone again, Arthur Tingley put his elbows on his grandfather's roll-top desk and pressed his palms against his forehead, squeezing his eyes tight shut. He sat that way, motionless, for a full ten minutes, then stirred, blinked around, and regarded with grim distaste the basket of morning mail. In it, unquestionably, would be indignant letters about inedible titbits, and a batch of cancellations.

Any ordinary business day of any business man is apt to have headaches, but before that Tuesday was past Tingley's amanuensis—an angular and tenacious girl of forty-three whose name was Berdine Pilt and whom he always called "my clerk" and never "my stenographer" or "my secretary"—became aware that he was setting an all-time record for growling, barking and snapping. She blamed it chiefly on the quinine, but surmised that the morning's callers had mysteriously made it worse; his ejaculations and comments, and the letters he dictated, offered no clue.

The room she occupied being divided from his by two partitions, she missed a good deal. She heard not a word, for instance, of the conference he had at half past two in the afternoon with Miss Yates and the sales manager, Sol Fry; nor had she cognizance of a peculiar expedition which he made precisely at four o'clock. It was brief and appeared to be surreptitious. He slipped out by the door through which Miss Yates had in the morning conducted Tecumseh Fox, walked fifteen paces down a partitioned corridor, stopped at an open door, glanced up and down the corridor, and dived within. He was in a long narrow room with female wearing apparel ranged along both walls and a partition down the middle, mostly coats disposed on hangers. Going straight to a worn coat with a muskrat collar, he glanced around again, warily, plunged his hand into the pocket of the coat and withdrew it again clutching a small covered glass jar, went back to the corridor and returned to his office. At that moment Berdine Pilt knocked on the other door with mail to sign, and he dropped the jar into a drawer of his desk and hastily shut it.

Berdine did know that there was something to be said to Phil Tingley when he came in at five o'clock, for she had been told to convey the message to the front; but since she went home at that time, along with everyone else on the premises except Miss Yates, who usually stayed in the factory until around six, she was divided from that interview by more than two partitions. She saw Phil's arrival a minute or so after five, but not his departure some forty minutes later; and eight subway miles separated her from what was perhaps the most surprising phenomenon of the day, a telephone conversation which occurred at a quarter to six, five minutes after Phil's departure.

Arthur Tingley scowled at a row of pigeonholes as he spoke:

"Buchanan four three oh one one? Is this you, Amy? This is your Uncle Arthur. I want—uh—I have—uh—a problem, and I want you to help me out.

Can you come here to the office at six—no, wait a
minute, damn it, that won't do—can you come at
seven o'clock? No no, not that. Not on the telephone.
No, I can't. Well, damn it, I'm asking you. All right,
I'm asking it as a favor—a family favor—my sister
was your mother, wasn't she? We can discuss that
when you come . . ."

Amy Duncan, in the living room of her apartment
on Grove Street, returned the phone to its cradle and
sat down on the sofa with an expression on her face of
disgusted bewilderment.

"That's a hot one," she told nobody aloud. "And I
said I'd go. I certainly have a head full of mush. I
should have told him to take his darned problem to
Miss Bonner the detective."

She sat there some time and then went to the
bathroom and took an aspirin. It had been a highly
unsatisfactory day. She had got up late and done
nothing. There had been nothing to do. She had plenty
of leisure now for rearranging the neck and letting
out the hem of the green dress, as she had intended to
do for her dining date, but now there was no date. At
a moment during the endless afternoon she had got
the dress out anyway and started ripping the hem,
but hadn't finished it. Nothing literally nothing, had
happened, with the single exception that around four
o'clock Tecumseh Fox had phoned to say that he
might have something to report in a day or two.

The friend who shared the apartment had flitted in
shortly after five, changed clothes like a cyclone, and
flitted out again. After taking the aspirin Amy drifted
into the bedroom, glanced into the mirror and saw
nothing encouraging there, and lay down on the bed

and closed her eyes. She stayed there over an hour. When she finally moved she jerked up with a quick start, looked at her watch, and scrambled to her feet.

"You poor simple-minded female," she said, again aloud in a tone of disgust, "if you think you don't know what you don't want to think about, don't think." Then abruptly, she burst into laughter. "Hey! That's good! I must tell—wah!"

Then in some haste she started to clean up and dress, choosing from the closet an old blue thing which she had never liked. There would be no time to eat, but she could do that later, and she wasn't hungry anyway. As near as she could tell through the windows, in the early November darkness, it was drizzling outdoors, but when she got to the street, finding that it was a cold windy rain, she decided on a taxi and was lucky enough to get one before reaching the corner. In front of the Tingley building on 26th Street she dismissed it and made a dive through the wet gusts for the entrance, pushed the door open, and entered.

But she stopped just inside, not closing the door, for there was no light. The dilapidated stairs led up into blackness. Then she remembered one of the countless inconveniences of the ancient place: there were no wall switches. She moved cautiously into the hall with both hands above her head groping in the air, found the chain, pulled it and got light, closed the outer door, and started up the stairs. The sound of her footsteps on the patient old boards penetrated into an encompassing silence. At the top she groped in the air again and pulled another chain, then crossed and opened the door to the anteroom. There was no light there either.

She stood motionless half a moment, and a shiver ran over her.

The shiver was a muscular reflex caused by a flash of panic along her nerves, but it was utterly uncalled for. The dead engulfing silence was certainly profound, but Uncle Arthur would not necessarily be stamping up and down, and there was no reason to suppose that any other noise-producing beings were in the building. As for the absence of light, there was nothing alarming about that; during her employment there Amy had once remarked that leaving after dark was like going through a series of stick-ups. Tingley's didn't believe in wasting electricity.

Nevertheless, she shivered. She even felt for an instant an almost uncontrollable impulse to shout her uncle's name, but succeeded in downing that weakness. She did, however, leave the door to the hall open; and she continued that tactic as she made her way, stopping to grope for more chains throughout her progress, through the maze of partitions which led her to the door that said THOMAS TINGLEY. There, finally, the chain had already been pulled; the door stood open and the room was light. As she entered a glance showed Amy that Tingley was not at his desk. She halted, started forward again, and—according to those who claim that consciousness is an essential of animate existence—there was no more Amy Duncan.

She returned to a state of being—no telling, for her then, how long after leaving it—in much the manner of a slippery thing pushing painfully through the slime at the bottom of a muddy river. The agony was so dull that it was not agony. For some moments she was still not in any real sense a live creature, but merely an incoherent and distant buzz of nerve impulses. Then something happened; namely, her eyes opened; but she hadn't quite reached the level of knowing it. Soon, though, she did; she groaned and made a mighty effort to lift herself with her arm as a lever; but her hand slipped and she was flat again just as enough consciousness returned for her to know that what her hand had slipped in was a pool of blood, and the object there on the floor an arm's length away was the face and throat of Uncle Arthur; and the throat. . . .

Chapter 4

She thought—if a numbed and blurred awareness can be called thought—that it was the shock of what she saw that was holding her paralyzed, but the contrary was the fact. Actually the shock gave her strength, in spite of the injury she had sustained, to twist away, pull herself to her knees, and crawl across the floor, skirting the pool of blood, to where the marble wash basin stood against the wall. Still on her knees, she reached to pull a towel from the rack, and with it, steadying herself with a shoulder against a leg of the basin, she wiped at the hand that had slipped in the pool. That action was necessitated by something more primitive than the will, it was instinctive; simply, there could not be blood on her hand. As she let the towel fall to the floor, there was revolt in her stomach. She rested her head against the rim of the basin, shut her eyes, and tried not to breathe. After an eternity she tried desperately to swallow saliva, and managed it. In another eternity she gripped the basin with both hands, pulled herself up, using all her strength, and was on her feet.

It remains problematical what she would have done then if her wits had been clear. It is charitable to her character and intellect to suppose that she would have gone to the telephone and called the police, and probably she would. But her wits were anything but clear. She was still more than half stunned. So she stood there awhile by the basin, gazing with widened but pain-dulled eyes at the body and its blood on the floor, and then relinquished her hold on the basin, found she could stay upright, and started to move. Her course was a wide circle around the obstruction on the floor and the burlap screen which stood there; she achieved it by making it a section of a polygon instead of an arc. At the door she leaned against the jamb to gather more strength. She knew now that there was something wrong with her head other than the shock of seeing Uncle Arthur on the floor with his throat cut, and, resting against the door, she put up her hand to feel and looked at her fingers, but apparently there was no open wound. Then she was driven on.

She would certainly never have made it to the street if anyone had pulled the chains of the lights she had left on as she entered, but no one had, so she reached that goal. It was still raining and she walked into it unheeding without wasting precious energy for closing the door behind her. On the two stone steps to the sidewalk she staggered and nearly fell, but regained her balance without going down, and started east. By now she had a dim feeling that there was something wrong with what she was doing, but its force was weak against the compelling necessity to keep going, keep going. She set her jaw, though that made the hurt in her head worse, and tried to walk faster and straighter. She crossed an avenue, came to another one, saw a taxi at the curb, and got in and told the driver 320 Grove Street.

Only there, at her destination, did she become
aware that she didn't have her bag containing her
purse. That made her, for the first time since she had
regained consciousness, really try to use her brain. It
was a pitiful attempt. The bag, of course, was there in
that place. It shouldn't be there. If it should turn out,
for any reason, to be advisable for her to conceal the
fact that she had been there—a point much too intri-
cate and abstruse to be given immediate consider-
ation—the bag not only shoudn't be there, it mustn't.
Then it had to be removed. The only person who could
or would remove it was herself. The only way she
could remove it was to go back and get it. She wasn't
going back. Her brain having completed that elemen-
tary but flawless performance, she asked the taxi
driver to come up to her apartment with her, got a
ten-dollar bill from a cache in her closet and paid him,
and, when he had departed, took the Westchester
phone book to the reading lamp, found the number
she sought, Croton Falls 8000, and called it.

She pulled a chair up to the table to sit and supported her head with her clenched fist as she talked:

"Hello! Mr. Fox? May I speak to him, please?" A
wait; she closed her eyes. "Hello! This is Amy
Duncan. No, I—I'm here at home. Something has happened. No, not here, it happened—I don't want to tell
you on the phone. No no, not that—something awful.
My head is only half working and I guess I'm not very
coherent—I know I have a terrible nerve—there's no
reason why you should except that there's no one else
I can ask—could you come right away? No, I can't on
the phone—I only half know what I'm saying—all
right. Yes, I know it will—I—all right, I'll be here—"

She dropped the phone on its cradle, sat there a
moment, and then braced her hands on the table and

got to her feet. The collar of the gray fur coat was wet against her neck. She got it off and hung it on the back of the chair, but when she put her hands up to remove her hat she staggered, swayed sidewise, crumpled into the sofa, and passed out again.

The first thing she knew, she smelled something disagreeable and irritating but familiar. Anesthetic? No. Ammonia. But why had she brought ammonia to bed with her? She opened her eyes. There was a man.

He asked, "Do you know me?"

"Certainly I do. Tecumseh Fox. But why—" She stirred.

He put his fingertips on her shoulders. "You'd better lie still. Do you remember phoning me?"

"Yes—I—"

"Just a minute. If you turn your eyes you can see Mr. Olson here. He had to let me in, and he needs to know whether I'm friend or enemy."

She moved her head, said ouch, and saw the janitor there looking worried. "It's all right, Eric," she said. "Mr. Fox is a friend. Thank you."

"But you—you look sick, Miss Duncan."

"I'll be all right. Thanks."

When the door had closed behind Mr. Olson, Fox got a glass from the table and proffered it. "Here, take a sip of this. Just enough for a spark until I know what floored you. I found it in the kitchen, so it's on the house."

The brandy lit a fire in her. She swallowed the other spoonful and let him take the glass. Her head dropped back to the cushion and a spasm passed over her from top to foot.

Fox's voice sounded like a roar to her, though in

fact it wasn't: "Before I used the ammonia I took off your hat and covered your legs and did a little detecting. You've been walking in the rain, you left your bag somewhere, you've been wiping blood from your hand, not very thoroughly, and someone hit you on the head with something."

She made an effort to hold her eyes open, and to speak. The brandy was burning. "How do you know they did?"

"There's a lump above your right ear the size of a lemon. Feel it yourself. Who hit you?"

"I don't know." She tried to concentrate. "I didn't even know I was hit."

"Where were you?"

"In Uncle Arthur's office. He—he's dead. He's there on the floor with his throat cut open—Oh, I—I—"

"Take it easy," said Fox sharply. The suggestion of a smile which was more or less continuously at the corners of his mouth had suddenly disappeared. "And keep your head still; we don't want you passing out again. Did you see your uncle dead on the floor with his throat cut?"

"Yes."

"When you arrived?"

"No. He wasn't there when I arrived—I mean I didn't see him—there was a light in the office and I walked in—I didn't see anybody or hear anybody—"

She stopped and Fox said, "Go ahead."

"That's all I know. When I came to and opened my eyes—my hand slipped when I went to lift myself up —and I saw it was blood and Uncle Arthur was there so close—"

"Just keep your voice calm. Go ahead."

"I crawled over to the wall and got a towel and wiped my hand—then I stood up—then when I could walk I went away. I knew something was wrong with my head but I was too dumb to realize what—"

"Dumb or numb. Did you come straight here?"

"I walked to an avenue—I think Eighth—and got a taxi."

"Did you phone me as soon as you got here?"

"Yes, right away."

"You phoned me at eight forty-two." Fox calculated. "Then you left there about ten after eight. What time did you get there?"

"At seven o'clock. Only I was late, maybe ten minutes late. Uncle Arthur phoned and asked me to come at seven, but I was late."

"Did you take a taxi?"

"Yes, it was raining."

"You left your bag there?"

"I must have—in the taxi I didn't have it."

"Why did your uncle ask you to come? What for?"

"I don't know. He said he had a problem—he asked it as a favor—a family favor, he said—if you'd give me a little more brandy."

He poured a small finger and handed it to her, and waited for it to go down.

"Did he say what the problem was about?"

"No."

"Did you think it was about the quinine?"

"I didn't see how it could be—I don't remember exactly what I thought."

"What time did he phone you?"

"I don't—wait, yes I do. I saw I'd have to leave in about an hour, so it was a little before six. Around a quarter to six."

"What did you do during that hour?"

"I went in the bedroom and lay down. I had a headache."

"Let me feel your head."

She let him. His competent fingertips, inserted through the strands of her brown hair, moved gently over and around the bump over her ear, then, with his eyes on her face, the fingers suddenly pressed firmly, and she winced and grimaced.

"Did that hurt much?"

"Well—enough."

"Sorry. I think you'll be all right. Excuse me for rushing things, but there's a possibility even now— did you make sure your uncle was dead?"

"Make sure—" She stared.

"Make sure he wasn't breathing or his heart beating."

"My God." Her tone was horror. "But he—no— what I saw—"

"All right. But the jugular had to be reached." Fox gazed down at her. "Why didn't you phone the police?"

"I couldn't. My head—I wasn't really conscious of what I was doing until I got outdoors—"

"I don't mean there. After you got back here. You knew I was sixty miles away and it would take me an hour and a half to get here. Why didn't you phone the police?"

She met his gaze. "Oh," she said. "I simply don't know. I guess I was afraid, but I don't know what I was afraid of. Right after I phoned you I tumbled here on the sofa. If you think—what I've told you is exactly the way it was—but if you think—"

"What do you want me to do?"

"Why, I—all I can say is, when I phoned you, it was awful and I was stunned and felt helpless—I don't know what you can do and of course there's no reason why you should do anything—"

Fox suddenly and surprisingly grinned. "Okay. You sound good to me." He stepped to the table, got out his notebook and found a page, pulled the phone across, and dialed a number. After a moment he spoke:

"Hello, Clem. 'Tec the Fox alias Fox the 'Tec. Greetings. Come out in the rain, please. No, but a little job that may be important. Come right away to 320 Grove Street apartment of Miss Amy Duncan, two flights up. I won't be here, but she will. Examine her head. First, attend to her—I'm sure there's no fracture. Second, determine if you are prepared to swear that she received a blow about three hours ago which knocked her cold. Third, take her to that hospital you try to boss and put her to bed. No, I didn't. When I hit ladies they land in China. Right away? Good. Many thanks and I'll see you tomorrow."

Fox shoved the phone back and turned. "So. That's Doctor Clement Vail and he'll be here within half an hour. Don't tell anyone where you're going. You'll be in better shape to converse with cops tomorrow than you are tonight. Doctor Vail is handsome and sympathetic, but don't tell anyone anything until you hear from me, which should be in the morning. This may be rough going, or there may be nothing to it as far as you're concerned. Even if we wanted to pretend you weren't there, which is rarely a good idea, we couldn't, with all your taxi rides and leaving your bag behind. Is there a catch lock on that door at Tingley's Titbits?"

"But you—you're not going there—"

"Somebody has to. Don't hold me up. Is the door locked?"

"No—I think I didn't even close it—it's open—"

"Good."

Fox picked up his coat and hat. Amy stammered:

"I don't know what to say—I mean, I had a nerve yesterday to ask you to help me, and now—"

"Forget it. I love to shine my light. Also, this is my chance to make the P. & B. vice-president no better than a dim and trivial memory. By the way, though you're minus your purse, apparently you're not broke. There's nine dollars and thirty cents on the table."

"I had some money here."

"Good for you. Remember, no talking until you hear from me. See you tomorrow."

He left her. Downstairs he found the janitor, to hand him a dollar and ask him to admit Dr. Vail. It was still raining, but his car was right in front. He had to make three turns to get to Seventh Avenue, where he headed north. If any of his friends or associates had been in the car, they would have felt a tingle of expectation at hearing him strike up the tune of the "Parade of the Wooden Soldiers." "Lah-de-dah, dum-dum, lah-de-dah, dum-dum," as the Wethersill rolled uptown, with the windshield wiper for a metronome.

In the neighborhood of the Tingley building the street was completely deserted, desolate in the driving rain. He parked squarely in front of the pedestrian entrance, unlocked the dash compartment and took out a pistol and a flashlight, slipping the former into his pocket and keeping the latter in his hand, and got out and darted across the sidewalk. But what he headed for was the dark tunnel of the cobbled driveway for trucks a little to the right of the entrance. The beam of the flashlight showed him that it was empty throughout its length, past the loading platform to the other end of the premises. He darted out again and up the two stone steps, found the door open as Amy had said, entered the building, and mounted the stairs, not needing the torch because the lights were on. In the anteroom he stood motionless for ten seconds, heard nothing whatever, and proceeded, with no effort to conceal his own noise. The doors were all standing open.

Two spaces inside Arthur Tingley's office, just beyond the edge of the burlap screen at his right, he stopped again. Taking Amy's story as she told it, it must have been just there that she had been struck. Considering the screen, that was all right. He circled the screen and directed his eyes downward.

A tightening of the muscles around his mouth and a breath intake through his nostrils somewhat quicker and deeper than common were his only visible reactions to what he saw. Though a glance was enough to make it more than probable that Amy had not, in her stunned daze, left her uncle to bleed slowly to death, he stepped around the area of the congealed liquid on the floor to bend over for a brief but conclusive examination. That done, he straightened up for a survey. For three minutes he stood, moving only his head and eyes, filing away a hundred details in the cabinet in his skull. The outstanding items were:

1. A bloody towel on the floor by the wash basin, sixteen inches from the wall.
2. Another bloody towel on the rim of the basin, to the right.

3. A long thin knife with a black composition handle on the floor between the body and the screen. In the factory that morning he had seen girls with similar knives, sharp as razors, slicing meat loaves.

4. Also on the floor, between the two front legs of the wash basin, a metal object nearly as big as his fist, in the form of a truncated cone, with a figure 2 in high relief on its side. That too, or its fellow, he had seen in the factory: a two-pound weight of an old-fashioned scale in the sauce room.

5. Farther away, out beyond the edge of the screen, a snakeskin bag—a woman's handbag.

When he moved, it was to kneel for a close inspection of the knife, without touching it; and the same for the metal weight. It was unnecessary to repeat the performance for the handbag: from his height he could see the chromium monogram, AD, at a corner of it. It, too, he left untouched; in fact, he touched nothing, as he toured the room, but he saw that someone else had touched a great many things, during what had apparently been a thorough search. Two drawers of the roll-top desk were standing open. Objects which, when he was there in the morning, had been neatly and compactly stacked on rows of shelves, were now disarranged and anything but neat. A pile of the trade journal, *The National Grocer*, had tumbled to chaos on the floor. The door of the enormous old safe was standing wide open. Arthur Tingley's hat was still on the little shelf above and to the left of the desk, but his coat, instead of being on the hanger which dangled from a hook beneath the shelf, as it should have been, was in a heap on the floor.

Fox noted these and many other evidences of a search, stood scowling in the middle of the room and muttered, "It's too damn bad I can't make a job of it," and departed.

It was still raining. Five minutes later, at 11:21 by his watch, he was in a phone booth in a drugstore at 28th and Broadway, speaking in the transmitter:

"All right, if the inspector isn't there I'll tell you about it. May I have your name, please? Sergeant Tepper? Thanks. You'd better write this down. Name: Arthur Tingley. Place: His office on the second floor of his place of business at Twenty-sixth Street and Tenth Avenue. He's there dead, murdered, throat cut. Let me finish, please. My name is Fox, Tecumseh Fox. That's right. Tell Inspector Damon I'll see him tomorrow—hold on and get this, will you?—I'll see him tomorrow and tell him where Amy Duncan is. Amy Duncan!"

He cut off loud remonstrances by hanging up, went out to his car and drove to the Hotel Vandermeer and asked the doorman, who greeted him as an old acquaintance, to have the car garaged. Inside the clerk greeted him similarly, but exhibited no surprise when he wrote "William Sherman" on the registration sheet.

He smiled at the clerk and said, "The police are after me, and they may even canvass the hotels, but I intend to sleep." He put a fingertip on the "William Sherman." "You can always trust the written word."

"Certainly, Mr. Fox." The clerk smiled back.

In a clean and comfortable room on the twelfth floor, Fox got his notebook from his pocket and flipped to a page, and arranged himself at ease in an upholstered chair next to the telephone. He stayed there half an hour, making a series of seven calls. The sixth was to his home in the country, to tell Mrs. Trimble that there would probably be an inquiry for him, and that he wasn't telling her where he was so she wouldn't know. The seventh was to the East End hospital, to tell Dr. Vail where he was, and to learn, as he did, that Miss Duncan had no serious injury, had been safely transported, and was fairly comfortable.

He undressed and went to bed a nudist.

Chapter 5

Though the detective bureaus of the New York City police force are by no means staffed exclusively by university graduates—a questionable fate which Scotland Yard in London seems to be headed for—neither does their personnel consist entirely of heavy-handed big-jawed low-brows. Inspector Damon of the Homicide Squad, for instance, while he is rather big-jawed, possesses fine sensitive hands, a wide well-sculptured brow, and eyes which might easily belong to a morose and pessimistic poet. His educated voice is rarely raised but has an extended repertory, as is desirable for a man who deals daily with all kinds from disintegrating dips to bereaved dowagers.

As he sat behind his desk at headquarters at eleven o'clock on Wednesday morning, speaking to a man seated opposite—a gray-haired man with the four buttons on his coat all buttoned and his hands folded in his lap in the manner traditional to parsons—his voice was merely businesslike:

"That's all for now, Mr. Fry, but you will of course keep yourself available. I have told Miss Yates that beginning at noon things can proceed as usual at the

Tingley premises, with the exception of Mr. Tingley's
room. We'll have two men in there day and night, and
nothing is to be touched, and certainly not removed,
without their approval. I am aware of your authority,
jointly with Miss Yates, as a trustee, and we'll cooperate all we can, but if there are any documents or
records in that room—"

"I told you there's none I need," Sol Fry rumbled
angrily. "The records of my department are where
they belong. But I don't care a Continental—"

"So you said. That's all. It will be the way I say for
the present—Allen, show Mr. Fry out and bring Fox
in."

A sergeant in uniform stepped forward to open
the door, and after another rumble or two Sol Fry
gave it up and went. In a moment Tecumseh Fox entered, crossed briskly to the desk, and stood.

"Good morning, Inspector," he said politely.

Damon grunted. As he sat looking up at the caller
his eyes were not only morose but also malign. After a
silence he extended a hand.

"All right, Fox, I'll shake, but by God. Sit down."

Fox sat. "You're going to find—" he began, but the
other cut him off:

"No, no. Try keeping quiet once. I'm going to make
a short speech. Do I ever bluster?"

"I've never heard you."

"You're not going to. Nor do I get nasty unnecessarily. But here is a statement of the minimum: you
and Miss Duncan together held up a murder investigation twelve hours. It's true you phoned last night,
but you concealed the vital witness, the one to start
with, and kept her from us until morning. What you
do around other parts of the country is none of my
business, but I warned you three years ago against

operating in New York City on the theory that when you're running bases the umpires go out for a drink. Have you seen the district attorney?"

Fox nodded. "I just came from there. He's as sore as a finger caught in a door."

"So am I. I think you're through in Manhattan."

"I'd call that bluster. Quiet bluster."

"I don't care what you call it."

"Have you finished your speech? I'd like to make one too."

"Go ahead, but make it brief."

"I will. At 8:42 in the evening I get a call from Miss Duncan asking me to come to her apartment. I arrive at 10:10 and find her unconscious with a lump on her skull. I revive her, question her, and phone for a doctor, telling him to take her to a hospital if that's where she ought to be. Thinking that Tingley may be lying in his office bleeding to death, I get there as quick as I can and find that he is dead and has been for a while. I notify the police at once. I phone the hospital and learn that Miss Duncan got a severe blow, is resting, and should not be disturbed. Early in the morning I go to the hospital, find that she is in good enough shape to talk, inform the police of her whereabouts—"

"And when I get there," Damon cut in dryly, "I find her surrounded by Nat Collins."

"Certainly. She had got knocked stiff alongside a murdered man she wasn't on good terms with. Do you take the position that you object to her having a lawyer? I shouldn't think so. To finish my speech, I then had a hasty breakfast and arrived at police headquarters at eight A.M., which is bright and early to be running bases. In your absence, I made a complete statement which was taken down by your subordinate, went by request to the district attorney's office, got your message to return here at eleven, and here I am. On that performance you can fence me out of New York? Try it."

"You kept vital information from us for twelve hours. At least eight hours. And maybe something worse. Why all the telephoning?"

"You mean last night?"

"Yes. Half the people we've talked to—"

"Five, Inspector. Only five. That couldn't possibly have done any harm. I merely told them that I wanted to make sure they would be at work at Tingley's this morning, as I wanted to talk with them again. I thought one of them might betray some interesting reaction."

"Did they?"

"No."

"Why did you pick on those five?"

"Because they were the five people who could most easily have put quinine in the mixing vats, and I was exploring the theory that Tingley had discovered the guilty one and got murdered as a result."

Damon grunted. "Is your theory based on facts?"

"No, sir, only possibilities. All the facts I possess are in that statement you have."

"You'd like to believe that the motive for murder was in that quinine business."

"Like to?" Fox's brows lifted. "It would be nice if a detective could choose a motive the way he does a pair of socks."

"But you'd like to believe that, because it would let Miss Duncan out."

"Now, come." Fox grinned. "She's already out."

"Do you think so? Then why Nat Collins? Who paid for the phone calls you made last night? Who are

you working for? And how did a set of her fingerprints, in exactly the right position, get on the handle
of the knife that cut Tingley's throat?"

Fox frowned, leaned forward, focused his gaze,
and demanded, "Huh?"

"They're there," said Damon succinctly. "We got
plenty of hers from that leather bag which you had
sense enough to leave where it was. I have asked her
about it, in the presence of her lawyer, and she denies
having touched the knife. Her explanation, of course,
is that while she was unconscious her hand was used
to make the impressions. Yours too, I suppose."

"You're stringing me, Inspector."

"No. I'm not. The prints were there."

"Have you arrested her?"

"No. But if we get a motive that will carry the
load—"

Fox continued to gaze, his brows drawing together, then leaned back in his chair. "Well," he said,
in an entirely new tone, "that's different. I knew you
don't like anyone getting under your feet on a murder
case, and I had decided not to annoy you on this one,
thinking Nat Collins was all and more than Miss
Duncan would need to make it as little unpleasant as
possible. I had supposed that she had walked in there
at a bad moment, and the murderer had conked her
merely to get away. But now—"

"Now?" Damon prompted.

"I'm afraid I'm going to be a nuisance after all. Of
all the snide tricks." Fox abruptly rose to his feet.
"Are you through with me?"

"About. For the present. I wanted to ask if you
have anything to add to this statement. Anything at
all."

"No. You think I know something, but you're wrong."

"Why do you say I think you know something?"

"Because you told me about those prints, thinking you might open a seam. But you're wrong. I'm starting from scratch. With your squad working on it already twelve hours, you know a devil of a lot more than I do. One of the things you know, I'd appreciate it very much if you'd tell me. Were Miss Duncan's prints on the two-pound weight?"

"No. Why should they be?"

"Because Tingley had been struck with it on the back of his skull."

"How do you know that?"

"Because I felt the place. The body was the only thing I touched. He was struck harder and in a more vulnerable spot than Miss Duncan, and I think there was a fracture. I doubt if I'm being helpful, but I'll finish. He was unconscious from the blow when his throat was cut. It would be next to impossible to slit a man's throat with a single clean deep stroke like that when he was on his feet and had his faculties. So—if you're nursing the fantasy that Miss Duncan did it— first she used the two-pound weight on him, and then the knife, and then she bopped herself on the side of the head with the weight. When she came to, she carefully wiped the weight clean but ignored the handle of the knife—"

The door opened to admit a uniformed policeman, who spoke to the inspector's inquiring eye:

"Phillip Tingley is here, sir."

"All right, one second." Damon regarded Fox gloomily. "You say you're going to be a nuisance. You know the rules, and you know you were out of bounds last night. I'm not forgetting that. You say you touched nothing in that room, but you went there alone before notifying us, and someone searched the place for something. You? I don't know. Did Miss Duncan send you there for something and you got it? I don't know. Did you learn something that you're not telling about that quinine business when you were there yesterday? I don't know. Where do I find you when I want you?"

"Home or Nat Collins's office." Fox added, turning to go, "Good luck, Inspector," and tramped out.

In an outer room where people were seated on a row of chairs against the wall, he stopped to tie a shoestring, and saw, from the corner of his eye, the policeman who had followed him out beckon to a bony-faced young man with brooding deep-set eyes. Having thus caught a glimpse of Philip Tingley for possible future needs, he proceeded to the corridor and the elevators.

On the second floor of the Tingley building on 26th Street, Sol Fry and G. Yates sat at a little table in the sauce room making a desultory lunch of Spiced Anchovies Number 34, potato chips, lettuce with dressing, and milk. They had done that for over thirty years, and Arthur Tingley had often eaten with them, as had his father before him.

"I don't think so," Sol Fry rumbled aggressively. "It's a black mystery and that's not at the bottom of it."

"You're wrong as usual," declared Miss Yates, with an equal aggressiveness in her unexpected soprano. "T. T. has had its ups and downs, like any other business, but there has never been anything disastrous, no real catastrophe, until this abominable quinine thing. And you'll find this was part of it. It ended in murder."

That too was following a hoary tradition, for Mr. Fry and Miss Yates had never been known to agree about anything whatever. The most frequent cause of dispute was the question of where the production department ended and the sales department began, or vice versa, but anything would do, and had, for a third of a century, done. Today, if they were to talk at all, the topic could not very well be anything but the tragedy that had put Tingley's Titbits in every news broadcast and on the front page of every paper, but that necessity was without effect on the tradition. So they continued to argue until, as Mr. Fry was taking the last potato chip, a voice suddenly startled them:

"How do you do. Lord, it smells good in here."

Fry grunted belligerently. Miss Yates demanded, "Where did you come from?"

"I've been wandering around." Tecumseh Fox approached sniffing, his hat in his hand. "Never smelled such a smell. Don't let me interrupt your lunch. Not to annoy the cop out front, I came in at the delivery entrance and up the back way."

"What do you want?"

"Information. Cooperation." Fox pulled an envelope from his pocket, extracted a sheet of paper, and handed it to Miss Yates. She took it and read it:

> *To anyone not unfriendly to me:*
> *This is my friend, Tecumseh*
> *Fox, who is trying to help me by*
> *discovering the truth.*
> *Amy Duncan*

She passed it across to Fry and surveyed Fox with a noncommittal stare. "So," she observed, "it was Amy that sent you here yesterday."

"In a way, yes." Fox pulled a third chair closer and sat down. "Her, plus my impertinent curiosity. But I'm no longer curious about the quinine, unless it appears that there's some connection between that and Tingley's death."

"I don't think so," said Fry.

"I do," said Miss Yates. "Why does Amy need your help?"

"Because of the circumstances, which the police regard as suspicious. She was there—she discovered the body—"

"Nonsense. Anyone who thinks Amy Duncan could have murdered her uncle—what motive did she have?"

"That's the question they're asking—beyond the fact that she didn't like him and had quarreled with him. But also, her fingerprints were on the handle of the knife that cut his throat."

They both stared. Sol Fry said, "My heavens!" Miss Yates snorted, "Who said so?"

"Oh, they're there all right," Fox asserted. "That's well outside the limits of police technique in a case like this. Of course they're aware that there's more than one way the prints could have got there, but it goes to explain why Miss Duncan needs a little help. Will you folks tell me a few things?"

"There's nothing I can tell you," Fry declared. "This thing is a black mystery."

"We'll brighten it up a bit," Fox smiled at him, "before we're through with it. Of course you've already told the police where you were yesterday from 5:45 to 8:15 P.M."

"I have."

"Would you mind telling me?"

"I mind it, yes, because I mind everything about it, but I'll tell you. I left here a few minutes after five and went to 23rd Street and Sixth Avenue to look at a radio I had seen advertised. I listened to it an hour and didn't like it. Then I walked to the 23rd Street ferry and crossed the river to my home in Jersey City. I got home about a quarter to eight and ate supper alone because my wife is an invalid and had already had hers. I went to bed at ten o'clock and had been asleep nearly two hours when you telephoned—"

"I'm sorry I woke you up, Mr. Fry. I apologize. I should think the tube would be much faster than the ferry."

"The police do too," Fry growled. "And I don't care what you think any more than I do what they think. I've been taking the ferry for forty-five years and it's fast enough for me."

"That's the Tingley spirit, all right," Fox agreed. He turned. "You don't have to monkey with ferries, do you, Miss Yates?"

She ignored the pleasantry. Having glanced at the clock, "It's five minutes to one," she stated, "and we're going to start three mixers."

Fox looked surprised. "Today?"

She nodded shortly. "Customers want their orders filled and people want to eat. Arthur would expect it. I told you yesterday, there hasn't been an order go out of here a day late since I was put in charge twenty-six years ago." Her voice had the timbre of pride. "If Arthur—" She stopped, and after a moment went on. "If he could send a message, I know what it would be. Stir the vats, pack the jars, fill the orders."

"Is that a sort of slogan?"

Sol Fry abruptly pushed back his chair, arose, rumbled, "I'll keep an eye on it," and marched out.

Miss Yates was on her feet.

"This is pretty urgent, you know," Fox remonstrated. "Miss Duncan is in a hole, and it may be a deep one, and time is important. If the quinine business furnished the motive for the murder, as you think, it's all over now. Can't you trust Mr. Fry? Do you have an idea he supplied the quinine?"

"Him?" Miss Yates was contemptuous. "He would as soon put arsenic in his own soup as quinine in a Tingley jar. He may be a doddering old fool, but the only life he lives is here. That's as true of him as it is of me." She sat down, leveled her dark eyes at him, and said tersely, "I usually leave here at six o'clock. Arthur Tingley was always the last one out. Yesterday as I was leaving he called me into his office, as he has frequently done since this trouble started. He said sales had fallen off nearly one fourth, and if it kept up he didn't see what could be done except to let P. & B. have it at their price. I said it was a shame and a crime if we couldn't protect our produce from ruination by a bunch of crooks. All he wanted was bucking up, and I bucked him up. I left at a quarter after six and went home to my apartment on 23rd Street, only seven minutes' walk from here. I took off my hat and coat and rubbers and put my umbrella in the bathtub to drain—"

"Thank you, Miss Yates, but I didn't ask for—"

"Very well. The police did," she said grimly, "and I thought you might like to know what they do. Usually I have dinner at Bellino's on 23rd Street, but it was raining and I was tired and dispirited, and I went home and ate sardines and cheese. At eight o'clock a friend of mine, Miss Cynthia Harley, came to play cribbage, which we do Tuesdays and Fridays, and stayed until half past ten. What else do you want me to tell you?"

"Cribbage?"

Her brows lifted. "Is anything wrong with cribbage?"

"Not at all." Fox smiled at her. "Only I am impressed at the pervasiveness of the Tingley spirit. Tell me, Miss Yates, who in this place dislikes Miss Duncan?"

"No one does that I know of, except Arthur Tingley. He did."

"The quarrel, I believe, when she left here, was about an employee who got into trouble and Tingley fired her."

Miss Yates nodded. "That was the final quarrel. They never did get along. For one thing, Amy was always standing up for Phil."

"His son Phil?"

"His adopted son. Phil's not a Tingley."

"Oh, I didn't know that. Adopted recently?"

"No. Twenty-four years ago, when he was four years old." Miss Yates stirred impatiently. "Are you expecting to help Amy by questions like this?"

"I don't know. I would like as much of the background as you'll take time to give me. Wasn't Tingley married?"

"Yes. But his wife died in childbirth and a year later he adopted Phil."

"Do you know who Phil's parents were?"

"No, but I know he came from some home up in the country somewhere."

"You said Miss Duncan was always standing up for him. Did he need standing up for?"

Miss Yates snorted. "He not only did, he does, and he always will. He's not a Tingley. He's an anarchist."

"Really? I thought anarchists were extinct. You don't mean he throws bombs, do you?"

"I mean," said Miss Yates in a tone that excluded levity, "that he condemns the social and economic structure. He disapproves of the kind of money we have. Because he was an adopted son, Arthur kept him on the payroll and let him have a drawing account of forty dollars a week which he never half earned. He was in Mr. Fry's department, with a territory in Brooklyn, mostly neighborhood stores and delicatessen shops. Why I said Amy was always standing up for him, Arthur kept jumping on him once or twice a week, and Amy kept saying there was no sense in it because Phil was what he was and yelling at him wouldn't help any. I suppose she was right, but Arthur was what he was too."

"I see," Fox screwed up his lips and looked thoughtful. "Do you know whether Tingley's disapproval of his adopted son led to any step as drastic as disinheritance? Do you know anything about his will?"

"I know all about it."

"You do? Will you tell me?"

"Certainly." Miss Yates was plainly desirous of erecting no needless obstructions to an early conclusion of this interview which was keeping her from the mixing vats. "The police know it, so why shouldn't you? I don't mind saying that some of us here were worried about what might happen in case of Arthur's death. Especially Mr. Fry and me. We knew Arthur had had the idea handed down to him of keeping the business exclusively Tingley, and that was why he adopted a son when his wife died and he vowed not to marry again. And we knew if it went to Phil, with the notions he had, there was no telling what would happen. But this morning, Mr. Austin, the attorney, told us about the will. It leaves everything to Phil, but takes control out of his hands by setting up a trust. Mr. Austin and Mr. Fry and I are the trustees. If Phil is married and has a child, it goes to the child at the age of twenty-one."

Fox grunted. "That's reaching into the future, all right. Did Phil know about the will?"

"I don't know."

"Did you or Mr. Fry?"

"I said we didn't. Not till this morning."

"So you and Mr. Fry, with Austin as a minority of one, are now in complete control of the business."

"Yes."

"All phases of it, including such details as salaries and emoluments—"

"That," said Miss Yates curtly, cutting him off, "I don't have to listen to, however willing I may be to help you get Amy out of trouble. I had to take it from the police, but not from you. Mr. Fry and I each get nine thousand dollars a year, and we're satisfied with it. He has put two sons and a daughter through college and I have over a hundred thousand dollars in government bonds and real estate. Neither of us cut Arthur Tingley's throat to get a raise in salary."

"I believe you," said Fox, smiling at her. "But I was thinking of the adopted son. Since control is entirely out of his hands, and if the trustees were so minded they could leave him with no income at all by a judicious manipulation of operating expenses, which include salaries, it seems unlikely that he murdered Tingley with an eye to personal profit. Unless he expected to inherit outright. Do you suppose he expected that?"

"I don't know."

"You don't know whether he knew the terms of the will or not."

"No."

"Would he be capable of murder?"

"I think he might be capable of anything. But as I told you, I think Arthur Tingley's death was in some way connected with the trouble we've been having with our product."

"You mean the quinine."

"Yes."

"Why do you think that?"

"Because I do. Because that's the only calamity we've ever had here and he was killed right in the middle of it, right here, right in his office."

Fox nodded. "You may be right," he admitted. "You realize, of course, that the police assume that the murderer was familiar with these premises. Not only did the knife come from the rack out there, but the weight—did the police tell you he was struck on the head by a two-pound weight which came from this room—from that scale there?"

"They tried to. But he wasn't."

"Huh?" Fox's head jerked and he stared. "He wasn't?"

"No. The weights that belong to that scale are all there. The one he was hit with belonged to a scale that old Thomas Tingley used when he started the business. Arthur kept it on his desk as a paper-weight."

"I didn't see it there yesterday, and I usually see things."

"It must have been there," Miss Yates declared. "It may have been under papers instead of on them. It usually was. Why, is that important?"

"I would call it vital," said Fox dryly. "I don't know about the police, but I have been regarding it as settled that the murderer was someone extremely familiar with this place, because he got that weight from this room before making the attack. But if the weight was right there on Tingley's desk—that spreads it out in all directions. As for the knife—anyone—even someone who had never been in the factory—might have expected to find a sharp knife in a titbits factory. And there was plenty of time to look, with Tingley on the floor unconscious, and it was in plain sight there on the rack. Was it?"

"Was it what?"

"In plain sight. Are the knives left on the racks at night?"

"Yes."

"Well. This certainly opens it up." Fox was frowning. "You say you left last evening at a quarter past six?"

"Yes."

"Tingley was in his office alone?"

"Yes."

"Did he say anything to you about expecting any caller or callers?"

"No."

"He didn't mention that he had phoned to ask Miss Duncan to come to see him?"

"No."

"Would you mind telling me exactly what he said—"

The question was cut off by the entrance of a woman about half Miss Yates's age in a working smock. She trotted up with the flurry of impending disaster on her face and in her gait. Fox knew her as Carrie Murphy, one of the five persons to whom he had telephoned at midnight, but without taking any notice of his presence she blurted at Miss Yates:

"Mr. Fry says the mix in vat three is too stiff and he's going to add oil!"

Miss Yates leaped from her chair and tore from the room, with Carrie Murphy at her heels.

Chapter 6

After rising to examine the two-pound weight which was there in its place in the row on the little shelf above the scale, and finding that it differed slightly in detail from one he had inspected on the floor of Tingley's office, Fox left the sauce room to stroll through the factory toward the front of the building. He saw no special evidence of grief on any faces of the girls and women working at the tables and benches and the various machines, but having himself met Arthur Tingley in the flesh, that did not seem to him shocking or even unexpected. Their curious glances at him as he passed along did, however, display an agreeably horrified suspense and perturbation, as well as an anticipatory gleam for the social supremacy they would have that evening among friends who worked for firms whose names were not in the papers at all, let alone in banner headlines on the front page.

There was a slight commotion at the far side of the huge room, where Miss Yates, backed up by Carrie Murphy, was confronting a defiant but obviously defeated Sol Fry. Fox sent a chuckle in that direction and went on.

A corridor led him past the open door of the long narrow room where the employees kept their wraps, and other doors as well. The last one on the right was closed. Fox turned the knob and pushed and breezed in. A broad-shouldered husky came at him, demanded angrily:

"Hey, what the hell?"

"My name's Tecumseh Fox."

"I don't care if it's Franklin D. La Guardia! On out!"

"I should think, shut up in here like this, you'd welcome an intruder once in a while to break the monotony."

Another man seated in Arthur Tingley's chair, with his feet resting on a newspaper on Arthur Tingley's desk, let out a growl, "Okay, go buy us a doormat with welcome on it. Run along."

"I just thought I'd save some steps by going through here to the front offices."

"Yeah. Do you want help?"

"No, thanks." Fox backed up for space. "The truth is, I'm drawn irresistibly to a room that has been searched by a murderer, as a bee is drawn to a flower. What if he didn't find what he wanted? I'd give a gross of Spiced Anchovies Number 34 to be in here alone for an hour. I see you've straightened up a little." *The National Grocer* had been returned to the shelf, and Tingley's coat was back on the hanger.

"He does want help," said the man at the desk. "Help him."

The husky made a forward movement. Fox backed out with sufficient alacrity, pulling the door with him.

He tried another door across the corridor and found himself in a medium-sized room with every inch of wall space occupied by rickety old wooden filing

cabinets and bookkeeping books on shelves. A young
woman with freckles and amazingly fine legs was filing papers, and a man who could have been the
brother of the one with rheumy eyes at the window in
the anteroom was nodding at a desk. Fox said pleasantly, "I'm a detective," and passed on through. He
had to invade four other rooms, opening and closing
five more doors, before he found the person he sought.
She regarded him with a startled and hostile expression from her seat at a typewriter desk, where apparently she had been doing nothing whatever, and there
was a redness around her eyes and her snub nose
which caused Fox to wonder if there was some grief
around after all.

"Good morning." He smiled at her, and added sympathetically, "You've been crying."

Berdine Pilt, who for sixteen years had nursed a
silent resentment at being called "my clerk" instead
of "my secretary," sniffed, picked up her handkerchief, and blew her nose with a total lack of inhibition
or restraint.

"I'm busy," she declared with finality.

"In circumstances like these it's a relief to have
something to do," said Fox, pulling up a chair.

He stayed with her half an hour, and got next to
nothing for it, though he displayed the note Amy
Duncan had armed him with. Miss Pilt professed admiration for Amy because during her brief stay at
Tingley's she had shown independence and spunk, and
affection for her because of her generous action in the
case of the fellow employee who had got into trouble,
but Miss Pilt was nevertheless indomitably discreet.
She took the position that since her room was separated from that of her employer by two partitions and
a corridor, and since she was not an eavesdropper, she

knew absolutely nothing of Tingley's confidential affairs, either business or personal. Nor could she be drawn into any speculation regarding the truth of the situation with respect to Phil, the adopted son; or an animosity in any quarter toward Amy Duncan which might have prompted the imprinting of her fingers on the handle of the knife; or whether the murder was in any way connected with the affair of the quinine. She did, however, furnish four items for the record:

1. She had left the premises, as usual, a few minutes after five o'clock, taken the subway to her home in the Bronx, and spent the evening there.
2. The redness came from weeping. She regretted and deplored the tragic death of Arthur Tingley, but the weeping was due to the fact that Mr. Fry and Miss Yates didn't like her and she didn't like them, and she would probably soon be out of a job at her age.
3. The only callers Tingley had seen on Tuesday, aside from the usual run of salesmen and such, had been a Mr. Brown, a tall well-dressed man around sixty whom Miss Pilt had never seen before and who had arrived a little after ten in the morning and had stayed nearly an hour; and Mr. Fox who had arrived at eleven. The tall well-dressed man was of course the one whom Fox had seen crossing the anteroom on his way out.
4. Shortly after Tingley returned from lunch, he had told Miss Pilt to tell the sales department that he wanted to see Phil when he came in with his day's orders and reports; and she had seen Phil enter his father's office a minute or so after five o'clock, as she was leaving. That, she admitted, had been unusual, but by no means unique.

Fox, after using her telephone to make a call to the East End Hospital, and hearing something, judging from his expression, which surprised and annoyed him, left Miss Pilt there with her empty machine at her empty desk. On his way out he tried his luck with the old man at the window in front, but soon discovered that if there was any pay ore in that vein it would take blasting to get down to it.

He drove east to Fifth Avenue and then uptown, maneuvered the car into a space on 41st Street that would barely hold it, went to a Bar & Grill that he knew and disposed of three ham sandwiches with lettuce and three cups of coffee. For his leisurely after-luncheon cigarette, he stood on the sidewalk and watched people go by. Then he walked around the corner to the entrance of a modest office building only sixty feet higher than the Great Pyramid, took an elevator to the thirtieth floor, entered a door which bore the inscription, NAT COLLINS, ATTORNEY-AT-LAW, and bade a sharp-featured alert-eyed woman good afternoon, calling her Miss Larabee. She said he was expected, and he went through two doors to a spacious corner chamber with two large windows on each of two sides. An appraisal of it would have depended on the focus of attention. If you limited your gaze to the five Van Goghs, all good and one famous, on the walls, you would have thought you were in a small private gallery; if to the rugs and furnishings, you would have said a blatantly luxurious office; if to the large healthy-looking man seated at the enormous carved desk, you still would not have suspected that you were in the sanctum of one of the three ablest criminal lawyers in New York.

Fox, however, looked at none of these, but at the

young woman in a chair at a corner of the desk. He
frowned at her and demanded:

"What's the idea? What did you leave the hospital
for?"

Amy Duncan had not only left the hospital, but
also had obviously been down to Grove Street. She
was wearing a tweed suit instead of the blue dress
she didn't like, a handbag of the same material as the
suit, and a little cockeyed felt hat. Her face, though,
with a general weariness and puffiness around the
eyes, displayed no corresponding rejuvenation. She
looked up at Fox and would have spoken, but the man
forestalled her:

"She's having an attack of autonomy. She doesn't
want me to make a living. She thinks he's armed without that's innocent within. She believes that virtue
needs no weapon and grows its own armor like a tur-
tle. I'm fired."

Fox tossed his coat and hat across to a chair,
propped his fundament against the edge of the desk,
folded his arms, and gazed down at her. "What's the
matter?"

"Why—nothing." Amy met his gaze. "Only my
head's reasonably clear again, and I see no reason
why you should—I mean especially engaging Mr. Collins—I never could afford to pay him anything like—"

"I hired him."

"I know, but how can I—I can't possibly accept—"

"Oh, you can't." Fox's tone was grim. "I don't
know whether you're scared because there are things
you know Collins and I will find out, or you're simply
a bum sport—"

"Neither one!" she denied hotly. "I'm not scared
and I'm not a bum sport!"

"No? Say you're not scared, then it's like this. You

walk into my car and get knocked down and have me take you home. You request free advice as from a brother detective. You let me look at your eyes from various angles and in various lights, knowing the probable effect on an observant and discriminating man. Confronted by a new and more urgent emergency, you yell for me through sixty miles of November rain. You let me get involved and committed to the point where I as good as tell Inspector Damon that the wraps are off. And now you begin whining about what you can't afford and what you can't accept—"

"I am not whining!"

"That's the impression you achieve, madam. Regarding the money to pay Collins, I've just sold a thousand shares of Vollmer Aircraft because I didn't want to make any more profit out of things that kill people, having already made too much. Collins doesn't care where his money comes from; he'll take it out of that. Regarding my time and effort, don't flatter yourself, in spite of your eyes. I'm an Arapaho on a trail, and I'm not eating or sleeping. Except at the usual times."

Collins laughed. Amy fluttered a hand. "I assure you—I know I asked you to help me, but I don't want you to think—"

"All right, I won't. Inspector Damon tells me that there's a set of your fingerprints on the handle of that knife."

"Yes, he—"

"And that you haven't any idea how they got there."

"I haven't."

"In my opinion," said Collins, "as I have told Miss Duncan, the person who put them there did so in a fit

of acute imbecility. I would use it on defense if the
state didn't."

Fox nodded. "That part of it's all right," he agreed,
"but it makes one thing certain—"

He stopped to let Nat Collins answer the phone.
After a moment Collins told the transmitter. "Wait a
minute," and turned to the others:

"This seems to be a cat in our alley. A man named
Leonard Cliff is here to see me. I'll take him to another room—"

"Excuse me," said Fox, "but I'd like to see him
myself. Let's all see him."

"Oh, no," Amy stammered, "it wouldn't be—I
don't want—"

They looked at her face. "Your color's better," said
Fox.

"Much better," said Collins. He spoke again to the
transmitter:

"Send Mr. Cliff in here."

Chapter 7

As the door opened and the visitor entered the room, he was—in appearance, bearing and manner—typically one of the younger set of top-flight New York business executives, soberly primed for an important interview. But four paces in he underwent a sudden metamorphosis. He halted abruptly, blood receded from his face, and his mouth opened and closed again without the emission of any sound. Then he started forward again, exclaimed, "Amy!" in a half-strangled tone in which distress and joy were mingled, and in that spurt reached the far corner of the desk, where he brought up with a second transformation, apparently caused by something he saw or didn't see in Amy's face, since he was looking nowhere else. He blushed furiously and looked de-railed.

Fox went to the rescue with a hand outstretched for a shake. "Mr. Cliff? I'm Tecumseh Fox. That sitting in the hand-carved monstrosity is Nat Collins."

The caller recovered enough aplomb to acknowl-edge the greetings passably, and addressed Amy:

"I thought you were in the hospital—I thought—I went there and they said you had gone home and I went there—" He moved some six inches nearer, which was about one tenth of the space between them. "I thought you—are you all right?"

"I'm perfectly all right, thank you," said Amy brightly.

"Well, that—" He stopped, the blush slowly receding, and then added in a weak and foolish tone better suited to a nitwit than an executive. "That's fine."

Fox helped out again. "Miss Duncan got a nasty crack, but suffered no serious injury. Did you come here to see her?"

"No, I—I didn't know she was here." Mr. Cliff was more of a man, talking to a man. "I came to see Mr. Collins. I intended to ask him where Miss Duncan was, but also I wanted to talk to him."

"Sit down," the lawyer invited, "and shoot."

"But I—" Cliff looked from him to Fox and back again, in obvious embarrassment. "It's rather confidential—"

"We're willing to remove ourselves," Fox offered. "Aren't we, Miss Duncan?"

"Certainly we are." Amy's tone, as she arose, indicated that she would like nothing better than to remove herself. "I certainly—Mr. Cliff's confidential affairs—certainly—"

"No!" The executive caught Fox's arm. "I didn't know I was interrupting—I don't want to interrupt—there's no reason—" Seeing he had Fox stopped, he moved to the chair at the other corner of the desk, sat, and said abruptly:

"I want to retain you, Mr. Collins."

Nat Collins beamed at him approvingly. "To a lawyer that phrase is poetry way above Keats or Shakespeare. May I ask to do what?"

"To defend me—uh—not defend me exactly. The

police have questioned me in connection with the death of Arthur Tingley. I am not of course suspected of murder, but they have learned that I was negotiating with him to buy his business for my company—I'm a vice-president of the Provisions and Beverages Corporation. Also they have asked me if I had knowledge of a recent attempt to damage the Tingley business by adulteration of its product. I did have knowledge of it, because the news had got around in the trade—by rumor as well as by channels of information of the sort that every large corporation keeps open. I knew no more about it, and certainly nothing of the murder. But even to be questioned by the police in such a connection is a little—disturbing. In the interest of my company as well as my own, I want—well, I want the advice and services if necessary of a good lawyer. I'd like to retain you for that."

Collins nodded. "To represent the corporation or you personally?"

"Why—I guess it would be better to make it me personally."

"It sounds more like a corporation concern."

"Well, maybe I can get them to share the expense." Cliff took a checkfold from one pocket and a pen from another. "It won't matter to you, I imagine, as long as you get paid." He opened the fold and uncovered the pen. "What shall I make this for a retainer? Five hundred? A thousand?"

"Wait a minute," the lawyer protested, "you're rushing me off my feet. We'd better have a little discussion before you subsidize me for servitude. I am already representing Miss Duncan in connection with the Tingley murder, and I would have to make it understood that in case of a conflict—"

"There's already a conflict," Fox interposed. "You're too late, Mr. Cliff."

"Too late?" Cliff turned to him with the expression of an executive meeting unexpected and vexatious obstruction.

"Yep. I'm sorry. Of course you intend to return later to inform Mr. Collins privately that what you really want to pay him for is to represent Miss Duncan, and that's already been arranged."

Amy made a noise. Nat Collins chuckled. Mr. Cliff, dealing with a man, said with spirit and composure, "You seem to know my intentions better than I do. On what basis do you make such a remarkable assertion—"

"Excuse me," Fox said brusquely, "but you're wasting time we might use for something else. Basis? As good as concrete. After chasing around the east end and Greenwich Village during business hours, you can't deny your energetic interest in Miss Duncan's welfare. How many firms of lawyers does your corporation have on its payroll? I suppose three or four, and good ones. In the kind of difficulty you describe, wouldn't you merely phone one of them to report for duty? Of course you would. And would you be volunteering to write your personal check instead of letting the company pay? Not unless you love stockholders with an unprecedented passion. Offering to toss in a thousand dollars of your own hard-earned dough for the honor of dear old P. & B.?" Fox shook his head. "Dismount. Honestly. No soap."

Collins was laughing,. "You see, Mr. Cliff, he's a detective."

"I—" Cliff stammered.

Amy, having already made noises, was on her feet

again. "This is utterly—" She left that unfinished. "It doesn't seem to matter that I—"

"Please, Miss Duncan," Fox entreated her. "Of course it matters. Sit down and count your blessings. The fact is, you are all that does seem to matter, which should be gratifying—I suppose, Mr. Cliff, you learned from the paper or radio that Nat Collins was acting for Miss Duncan, and you knew his fees are outrageous and her resources limited. As I say, you're too late; that has been taken care of; but you can help out some in another way, if you will. What were you and Dol Bonner talking about in Rusterman's Bar— please, Miss Duncan, sit down and relax—last Saturday afternoon?"

Mr. Cliff gawked at him. A frown creased his brow. "What the devil—"

"I assure you it's material, competent, and relevant. Miss Duncan: do you want Mr. Cliff to tell us what he was discussing with Miss Bonner?"

"No," Amy blurted.

Fox glared at her. "Please don't be a nincompoop. All aspects of this affair are going to have to be cleared up, whether we like it or not. Use your head, which was not fractured. Do we want him to tell us?"

"Yes," Amy said.

"All right," Fox turned to the executive, "*she* wants you to tell us."

Cliff looked at Amy. "You do?"

"Yes, I—if you feel like it."

Cliff said to Fox, "We were discussing a business matter."

Fox shook his head. "We need more. Doubtless you have learned from the press that Miss Duncan is Arthur Tingley's niece and was once employed by him —that was her connection with that place. Tingley engaged Dol Bonner to investigate the quinine in his titbits, with a conjecture, among others, that you or your firm had a hand in it. He learned that you had been seen in confidential conversation with Bonner, and feared that she was double-crossing him. You can tell us whether she was or not."

Cliff looked wary. "I fail to see what that has to do with Miss Duncan."

"That's another story, and for the present beside the point. It certainly had to do with Arthur Tingley, who was murdered, and with you."

"But you—" Cliff screwed up his lips. "You are, presumably, merely trying to protect Miss Duncan from—unpleasantness."

"Right. And it may turn out that the only way to do that is to discover who killed Tingley."

"God knows I didn't. And I had nothing to do with the adulteration of his product, either."

"Good. But your talk with Miss Bonner?"

Cliff looked at him, at Amy, at the lawyer, and back at Fox. He laughed shortly. "It could be funny, I suppose. You say Tingley hired Bonner to investigate the quinine. As you know, I wanted to buy Tingley's Titbits. It's the finest product in that line, with the best and biggest and oldest reputation, and it would have filled a gap for us. I knew Tingley would sooner or later take the hook, they always do. Then I heard that Consolidated Cereals was trying to butt in, and then came the news of the adulteration. I suspected C. C., knowing how they work. I thought I knew how to get a line on it, but it required some delicate doing. I telephoned Miss Bonner. I didn't want to go to her office, or her coming to mine, so we arranged to meet at Rusterman's to discuss it."

"Were you acquainted with her?"

"No. I had never met her."

"How did you happen to pick her?"

"I had heard of her, and this seemed to be her sort of job. She did some work for a friend of mine once." The executive glanced around. "I am counting on your regarding this information as strictly confidential."

"You can. And did Miss Bonner undertake—what is it, Miss Duncan?"

"Nothing," Amy declared. "Nothing!"

"You seemed to be speaking."

"No, I—I guess I coughed—of course I'm glad—"

"I suppose you mean that you're glad that your uncle would be glad to know that Miss Bonner was not double-crossing him, and that her meeting with Mr. Cliff was perfectly proper, and that Mr. Cliff was not putting quinine in his liver—"

"Yes—of course—"

"Of course. But don't overdo it. There's a new iris out—I have a clump of it up at my place—named Rosy Wings. Your face reminds me of a bud of Rosy Wings just bursting into flower. I'm glad you're glad, but there's still an unsolved murder, and the police won't be nearly as much impressed—"

"My God!" Mr. Cliff ejaculated as one who had just emerged from a noisome cavern into a sunny day. "That was all—your uncle thought I—he told you— you thought I—" He was out of his chair and across intervening space, and had one of her hands. "Amy!"

"Well, I—Leonard—I—"

They gazed at each other, with Nat Collins regarding them quizzically and Fox dubiously. Cliff murmured something at her and she murmured back, and they were both smiling.

Collins said, "I have two hard cases to bone up on.

I take it, Miss Duncan, that you accept Mr. Cliff's
statement without discount."

"She'd better," Cliff declared, "after suspecting
me of such a low-down trick as adulterating a compet-
itor's product. Good lord!" He stayed by Amy's chair,
and spoke to her: "May I take you home? Are you
through here?"

"No," said Fox, "she isn't. I want to ask her some
things."

Cliff returned to his chair and sat down. "Go
ahead."

Fox shook his head. "Confidential things. You can
wait out front if you want to, but it will be a long
wait."

"But with Miss Duncan's permission—you understand that I'm not claiming any right—"

"It wouldn't do you any good," Fox said shortly,
"if you did. Miss Duncan is under the suspicion of the
police in a murder case. So are you and some other
people. I am acting on the assumption that she is innocent, but on no similar assumption regarding anyone
else. If you were a detective working for her you
would do the same. So we won't get personal and you
can wait in front as long as you want to. All right?"

Cliff's face did not give the impression of acquies-
cence that it was all right, but he rose to his feet. "I
won't quarrel about it," he told Fox, "because I owe
you something. I certainly do. Also I have a fact to
give you which I have already given the police. Tingley phoned me yesterday afternoon and made an appointment to see me at ten o'clock this morning."

Nat Collins looked interested. Fox said, "Thanks.
What time did he phone?"

"At twenty to six. Just before I left the office."

"What did he say?"

"Just that he wanted to see me, and we made an appointment. He had never phoned me before, our communication had all been on my initiative, and I was pleased because I thought it meant that he was ready to make terms, but he didn't say so. He was curt and anything but amiable, but under the circumstances that was only natural."

"You thought he was surrendering."

"If you want to call it that. I thought he was prepared to make a deal that would be profitable for both sides."

Fox grunted. "It took a lot of quinine to get him into that frame of mind. I'm not saying that you furnished the quinine. By the way, you say you left your office at twenty to six. Would you mind telling me where you spent the next two hours and a half?"

The trite and routine question produced an effect. Cliff's eyes altered their focus for a fleeting glance toward the opposite corner of the desk, and his face changed color, faintly but perceptibly to an alert regard.

"Yes," he said, "I would."

"You mean you'd mind?"

"Yes."

"You mean you refuse?"

"Yes."

Fox shrugged. "Since the cops have questioned you, you certainly had to tell them. But suit yourself."

"I didn't tell the cops. I refused to. I told them that instead of inventing something about going for a walk or going to a movie, I preferred to state that from six to nine Tuesday evening I was on personal confidential business which I declined to disclose."

"I see." Fox smiled at him. "Maybe you'd better give Nat Collins a retainer after all."

"I believe I'll be able to keep afloat, Mr. Fox. So you're Tecumseh Fox. Well, as I say, I owe you something." Cliff looked at Amy. "May I wait for you and take you home?"

Their eyes met. "Why," she said, "it may be a long wait—"

"I don't care if it's a year."

"Well—of course a girl loves attention—"

"I'll be waiting," he said, and marched out.

After the door was closed, Fox cleared his throat to address Amy, but she spoke first.

"I want to kiss you," she said, "on the mouth."

"Come ahead."

"But I can't. I think I'm part Puritan. I'll bet I'm blushing. Or else I regard kisses as dissolute, which is so darned old-fashioned it makes me furious, but I can't help it. Only I really do want to kiss you."

Fox got up and crossed over, bent and kissed her proficiently on the lips without skimping, and returned to his chair.

"A little domestic but nice," Nat Collins allowed. "Now for God's sake let's line up a few—Come in!"

It was Miss Larabee. She advanced to the desk, handed Collins an envelope, and announced, "By special delivery five minutes ago. And Mr. Philip Tingley is here."

"Ask him to wait. If he gets restless, soothe him. If he gets too restless, send him in."

Miss Larabee went. Collins, regarding the inscription on the envelope, grunted, "Personal *and* important," and reached for a knife and slit the flap. Extracting a sheet of paper, he unfolded it and read it with a frown.

He glanced up at the others. "From our old friend John Henry Anonymous. As usual, he forgot to sign

it. Cheap envelope, cheap paper, typewritten by one
who knows how to spell and punctuate. Marked at
Station F at three P.M. today. I'll read it to you:

" 'Tuesday evening, twenty minutes after
Amy Duncan's arrival at Tingley's, which
would make it seven thirty since she arrived at
seven ten, a black or dark-blue limousine
stopped there. It was dark and rainy. The
driver got out and held an umbrella over another man as he crossed the sidewalk to the
entrance, then the driver went back to his seat.
In five minutes the man came out again, ran
across the sidewalk and climbed in, and the car
left. The license was OJ55.

" 'Five minutes later, at seven forty, a man
approached the entrance and went in. He had
on a raincoat with a hat with a turned-down
brim, and came from the east. He was inside a
little longer than the first man, maybe seven or
eight minutes. When he came out he hesitated
there a moment and then walked rapidly west.

" 'Proof of the reliability of this information:
When Miss Duncan left, a little after eight, she
stumbled on the second step and nearly fell,
and stood holding to the rail for thirty seconds
before she went on. The times and intervals
are approximate, but fairly accurate.' "

Collins looked at Amy. "Of course you did. Stum-
ble on the step and stand holding the rail. Otherwise
John Henry wouldn't have tacked on that embellish-
ment."

Fox, scowling, reached across the desk. "Let me
see that thing."

"I'm not sure," said Amy, concentrating. "My head was so dazed I'm not very sure about anything. But then—" Suddenly she straightened. "Someone was there watching! Dol Bonner was having me tailed!"

Fox, folding the sheet of paper, grunted. "Or the cop on the beat saw your eyes as you went in," he said dryly. "May I borrow this awhile?"

Collins nodded. He had reached for his phone and made a request to it, and presently he spoke:

"Bill? Nat. Love and kisses. Will you do me a little favor with the speed of light? Regarding a careless automobile, motor vehicle to you. New York license OJ55, whose is that? Call my office. Much obliged."

He leaned back and eyed Fox. "Well, what is it? I don't see how it can very well be a nut, with that about Miss Duncan stumbling. Do you?"

"Not a nut," Fox agreed. "I'll have to do some work on it, which of course will start with the owner of that license number. It's fairly certain that whoever wrote it was there when Miss Duncan left the building, probably in the tunnel of the driveway or she would have seen him. He was close enough to see a hat brim turned down and a license number, if he's not a liar. It's also certain that he's a trained writer— I'd say a newspaper man. Did you notice it?"

"Notice what?"

"There's no 'I' in it. Any ordinary person would have put in at least half a dozen. He was describing something he himself had seen, his own experience. Elimination of the 'I' from a recital of a personal experience requires training and acquired discipline. 'I couldn't see distinctly because it was dark and rainy.' That's the natural way to put it. Other places the same. It's a simple enough trick, but if you haven't learned it you just don't do it."

"You're right," Amy declared. "One of the operatives at Bonner and Raffray was on the *Herald Tribune* over a year."

"No, really?" Fox was sarcastic. "For the present, Miss Duncan, you'd better forget you're a detective. You have sentiments involved that tend to thwart the inductive process. You'll never forgive Dol Bonner for drinking a cocktail—"

"That isn't true!" Amy denied indignantly. "Just because I permitted you to kiss me—"

"Permitted? Ha!"

"Be quiet!" Nat Collins told them. The telephone had buzzed and he was at it. After a short conversation, from his end mostly growls, he hung up and made a face at Fox.

"He's a trained writer, all right. Fiction writer. There is no OJ55. There's no OJ at all with less than three figures."

Chapter 8

They looked at each other. No pertinent comment appeared to be forthcoming.

Finally Collins addressed Amy: "We ought to know if you stumbled on that step or not."

"She probably did." Fox tapped his breast over the pocket where he had put the paper. "I'll fiddle around with this in my spare time. What about Philip Tingley? Did you send for him or is he a volunteer?"

"I sent for him. I prodded Miss Duncan on the probable reason why her uncle phoned to ask her to come to see him. She doesn't know. She doesn't see how it could possibly have been in connection with the quinine thing. As a wild guess, the best she can do is that it might have been something about her cousin Phil. Tingley and his adopted son used to have frequent clashes, and Miss Duncan took Phil's side. She thinks Tingley had an exaggerated idea of her influence with Phil, because he once came down from his perch and appealed to her to use it to make him a better boy. So I got in touch with him and asked him to drop in."

"All right, let's take a look at him. May I have the overture?"

"Help yourself."

Collins used the phone for a message to Miss Larabee, and after a moment Philip Tingley was ushered in. Tall and ungainly and bony, dressed conceivably for a bread line, his hollow cheeks and the sagging corners of his mouth might have been attributed, by one who had never seen him before, to the shock and strain of the current casualty. He greeted Amy composedly, with a piercing glance from his deep-set eyes, allowing Collins and Fox, introduced, to grasp his bony fingers, and lowering himself into the chair that had been vacated by Leonard Cliff.

Amy said nervously, as one impelled to speak without having any specific communication to make, "It's ghastly, isn't it, Phil?"

"Not particularly," declared the last Tingley who was not a Tingley. "The death of one economically useless man, even in such an abhorrent manner, is regrettable only in a very restricted sense. If he had been my father I might feel differently. As it is, I don't feel."

"I congratulate you," said Fox cheerfully. "Not many people ever achieve that philosophic detachment toward death. You're not faking it, are you?"

"Why the deuce would I fake it?"

"I don't know. I suppose you wouldn't; you'd be more apt to fake distress and woe, which is often done. Do you feel equally indifferent to the fate of your cousin?"

"My cousin?" Phil frowned in puzzlement. "Oh— you mean Amy. I do not. I rarely form personal attachments, but she is the only woman I have ever proposed marriage to."

"Phil!" Amy protested. "You were only talking."

He shook his head. "No, I meant it. I had decided I

wanted to marry you. Of course I'm glad now I didn't, because it would have interfered."

"That was some time ago?" Fox inquired.

"That was in May and June, 1935."

"I see. It was the season of the year that unnerved you. But you are still well-disposed toward her? I ask because she needs a little friendly help. Did you know that your father—your foster father—phoned her yesterday to ask her to come to see him?"

"No. Did he? I don't think it was mentioned in the *Times*. I read only the *Times*."

"Well, he did. He phoned at a quarter to six, speaking of a problem on which he needed her assistance, and asked her as a family favor to be at his office at seven. That's why she went there. But the police have only her word as evidence that she received that phone call, and corroboration would help a lot. We have considered the possibility, among others, that the problem he spoke of was connected in some way with you."

"Why do you assume that?"

"Not assume it. Admit it as a possibility."

"Very well," Phil conceded, "it's a possibility."

"Thank you. But can't you make it more than that? Had any—uh—discussion between you and your father recently become acute?"

"Our quarrel was always acute. Chronic and acute both."

"But did it, between three o'clock Monday and six o'clock yesterday afternoon, reach a new crisis?"

"No."

"It didn't?" Fox smiled at him. "The reason I specify those hours is because Miss Duncan called on your father Monday afternoon, and when she left him, about half past three, his attitude was uncompromis-

ingly hostile and certainly didn't indicate that he was
about to ask her a favor. But at a quarter to six Tuesday he did telephone to ask her a favor. It would be
helpful if we could establish that in the interim something occurred to account for that. You realize, don't
you, that it would be extremely helpful to your
cousin?"

"Yes, I realize that."

"But you can't fill it in for us."

"No, I can't."

"Your father sent word for you to go to his office,
at five o'clock yesterday, and you went. What was
that about?"

Phil compressed his lips, thereby counteracting
most of the drooping effect at the corners. "That," he
said. He moved in his chair for an easier position.
"You sound like a police parrot. They asked about that
too. I understood you were merely defending Amy's
position in this."

"I am. Protecting the flanks as well as the front
and rear. If you'll tell us what you and your father
said to each other yesterday it might give us a peg to
hang that phone call on."

"We said what we always said."

"With no novel variations?"

"No." Phil was frowning at the necessity for touching upon a highly distasteful subject. "It was enough
without variations. He was chronically enraged at me
because I had brains enough to see the criminal futility and cachexia of the orthodox capitalist economy
and finance, and because I wouldn't immolate my
brains on the tottering altar of the petty business that
bounded his horizon. I was equally enraged, though I
controlled it better than he did, because he could easily have afforded to contribute considerable sums to

the cause I had embraced, the purification and rejuve-
nescence of world economy, and he refused. He paid
me a mere pittance for my work as a salesman. Forty
dollars a week. I live on fifteen and give the remain-
der to the cause. It pays for printing—"

He broke off abruptly and leveled his eyes at
Amy. "By the way. That pamphlet I gave you. You
gave it to the police. Did you read it?"

"To the police?" Amy looked bewildered. "But I
didn't—Oh! Of course. It was in my bag—that I left
there—"

"May I ask what pamphlet?" Fox got in.

"Womon Bulletin Number Twenty-six." Phil surveyed him. "I presume you have heard of Womon?"

"I'm sorry, but I haven't, unless it's a new pronun-
ciation—"

"No. It's Womon." Phil spelled it. "It will remove
the world's economic cancer. It stands for Work-
Money. Its central and revolutionary doctrine is that
all money must be based on the median potential of
man labor calculated by—"

"Excuse me. Is that the cause you are devoted
to?"

"Yes."

"Then you're not an anarchist?"

"Good God." Phil's tone was of unutterable disgust. "Where did you get that idea?"

"No matter." Fox waved it aside. "You say you
live on fifteen dollars a week. But of course you live at
your father's home."

"No, I don't. I moved out two years ago. In addition to all the rest of it, it was a constant battle there
to keep from playing bridge."

"May I have your address, in case—"

"Certainly. Nine-fourteen East 29th. There is no phone. Four flights up in the rear."

The phone buzzed and Nat Collins said, "Excuse me," and reached for it. He said, "Nat Collins speaking," and for something like twenty seconds merely listened; then he spoke again: "Hello! Hello? Hello hello?" He hung up and pushed the phone back, reached for a scratch pad and pencil, scribbled rapidly, tore the page off and handed it to Fox.

"A lead on that accident case," he said. "Follow it up when you get a chance."

Fox read the sprawling words:

A man disguising his voice said: "The man in a raincoat who entered Tingley's at 7:40 last night was Philip Tingley. This is not absolutely positive, but 100 to 1."

"Thanks," Fox nodded. "I may be able to get at it tomorrow." He stuck the paper in his pocket, and smiled at Phil. "Well, Mr. Tingley, I'm sorry you can't help us out with a motive for that phone call to Miss Duncan. I understand your talk with your father began shortly after five o'clock?"

"That's right."

"Would you mind telling me how long it lasted?"

"Not at all. Until twenty minutes to six."

"What did you do then?"

"I walked to Broadway and ate something in an Automat, and then went to 38th Street and Sixth Avenue, where we have a little office."

"We?"

"Womon."

"Oh. Do you often go there in the evening?"

"Nearly every day. I give all the money and time I

can spare. I left there around seven with a bundle of throwaways advertising a meeting we're going to have, and handed them out on 42nd Street. I got back there a little after eight and stayed until ten o'clock, when we close the office."

"So from seven to eight you were on 42nd Street handing out throwaways."

"That's right."

"Wasn't it raining? You did that in the rain?"

"Certainly. That's the best time for it. People collect in entrances and doorways and you have a bigger percentage of takes." Phil's mouth twisted. "If you're trying to get Amy out of trouble by getting me in, I don't think it will work."

"You mean you don't care to be implicated in the murder of your foster father."

"I not only don't care to be, I'm not going to be."

"Well, that's a strong position if you can hold it. Don't forget, though, that you have one bad weak spot: you are Arthur Tingley's heir."

"Heir?" The curl of Phil's lip was the next thing to a snarl. "You call it heir? With the business, such as it is, in a trust controlled by three decrepit relics?"

"The business is good enough for a three-hundred-thousand-dollar cash offer. And I suppose Tingley had other property besides the business, didn't he?"

"He did," said Phil bitterly. "And the whole works is locked up in that trust. Even his house and furniture."

"Were you aware of the contents of his will?"

"You bet I was. That was his favorite club to threaten and coerce me with."

"It must have been very disagreeable." Fox, looking sympathetic, arose to his feet. "Thank you very much, Mr. Tingley, though you didn't give us much."

He crossed to get his coat and hat. "Those things I want to ask you, Miss Duncan, they'll have to wait. I'll get in touch with you in the morning. See you later, Nat." He turned to go, but was halted by a voice:

"Here, wait a minute!" Phil Tingley pulled something from his pocket and extended it in his hand. "That's the Womon Statement of the Basic Requirements of a World Economy. Read it over. I'll send you a set of our bulletins—"

"Much obliged. *Very* much obliged." Fox took it and strode out.

Though he seemed to be in a hurry, he halted abruptly in the front room. Leonard Cliff was in a chair against the wall, reading an evening paper. Fox crossed to where Miss Larabee sat at her desk, and bent down to her as if the recent little episode with Miss Duncan had been habit-forming; but instead of kissing her he merely murmured in her ear:

"Has he been here all the time?"

Miss Larabee was apparently averse to whispering or murmuring in a man's ear. With no hesitation or change of expression, she swiveled to her typewriter, twirled in a sheet of paper, typed on it, and twirled it out again and handed it to Fox. He read it:

20 min. ago he asked where the men's room was and went out. Returned in about 10 min. with a newspaper, so he must have gone to the street floor.

"Thanks." Fox folded the paper and stuck it in his pocket. "I'll let you know if I have news." He stepped across to where Leonard Cliff sat.

"Mr. Cliff. You said in there, regarding the adulteration of the Tingley product, that you suspected

Consolidated Cereals because you knew how they worked."

Cliff, his newspaper lowered, nodded. "I know I did. I was indiscreet. But you promised to treat it as confidential."

"I will. That is, I won't disclose it where it isn't already known. In a conversation I had with Arthur Tingley on Monday, he too mentioned Consolidated Cereals. Are they major competitors of yours?"

"Not yet. But they—" Cliff stopped, then shrugged and went on. "After all, anybody in the trade could tell you. About a year ago Guthrie Judd of the Metropolitan Trust closed in on Consolidated Cereals and took it over. For the bank, of course. Do you know Judd?"

"No, but I've heard tell."

"Then I don't need to tell you. When I said I knew how C. C. works, I meant I knew how Guthrie Judd works."

"I see. Will you be at your office tomorrow?"

"Certainly."

"I may be dropping in. Much obliged."

Fox departed, descended to the street—where the early November darkness had already made it night—walked and dodged briskly to Madison Avenue and six blocks north, entered the lobby of another office building, and consulted the directory panel. Taking an elevator, he got out at the 32nd floor, and down a long corridor found a door with the inscription:

BONNER & RAFFRAY
DETECTIVES

Entering, he was in a small and handsome ante-room that was the antithesis of the one at Tingley's

Titbits. The walls were greenish cream, the lighting indirect, the floor's rubber tiling dark maroon; chairs and a small table and a garment rack were of red and black lacquer with chromium trim. There was no one there. Fox glanced around, and as he did so a door from an inner room opened and Dol Bonner came through, with coat, hat and gloves on.

"Just in time," said Fox. "I was afraid I'd miss you."

She smiled without warmth. "I'm honored." Her yellow-brown alert eyes met his. "I'm sorry—I have an appointment—"

"So have I, so I won't keep you. Nice shiny place you have here. What were you and Leonard Cliff discussing at Rusterman's Bar last Saturday afternoon?"

"Really." Her smile showed, if not more warmth, more amusement. "That's amazing. Do you get results like that?"

"When I have a good lever I do." Fox smiled back at her. "As I have now. It would be cozier to sit down and chat and lead up to it, but we're both in a hurry. The idea is, Cliff has told me his version of that conversation, and I'm getting yours to check up on him. You know the routine."

"Yes, but I make better use of it." The gleam in her eyes was certainly amusement. "Tecumseh Fox? You ought to be ashamed of yourself. Who do you think I am, the downstairs maid that answered the phone call?"

"Nope. But you're going to tell me. This isn't your murder case, so why not stay out of it? It will be an awful nuisance if you get in—I mean for you. You may regard it as proper and ethical to let A hire you to investigate B, and then let B hire you to investigate C, but you know how the police are. They'll get suspicious and when they're suspicious they're obnoxious. Their smallest suspicion will be that you were double-crossing A, and maybe you were until he got murdered. I'm not interested in that, but I want what I asked for. Otherwise, and immediately because I can't afford to wait, it's Inspector Damon on the telephone, and orders to bring you in dead or alive, and all the questioning and please sign this statement and be here again in the morning and don't leave the jurisdiction—"

"Damn you," Miss Bonner said. The amusement was gone. "You can't do it. How could you account for having it?"

"Easy. Use your head. I've already told you that I have it from Cliff and I'm only checking. Don't my A, B and C prove it?"

"I wasn't double-crossing Tingley."

"Good. Had you ever met or seen Cliff before Saturday?"

"No." Miss Bonner swallowed. "Damn you. He phoned the office and we arranged to meet at Rusterman's. I thought I might get a break on the job I was doing for Tingley, but when I found out what he wanted I saw no reason why I couldn't take his job too. It couldn't harm Tingley any, and neither could it harm Cliff if he was on the level—"

"What did he want?"

"He suspected that Consolidated Cereals was responsible for the trouble at Tingley's, and he wanted me to investigate and get proof if possible. The reasons he wanted it were, first, he expected to buy Tingley's and didn't want the property depreciated, and second, he wanted to expose Consolidated Cereals."

"Did he mention anyone specially?"

"Yes. Guthrie Judd of the Metropolitan Trust. They recently took over Consolidated Cereals."

"Was there anything else he wanted you to do?"

"No."

"Did you tell him you were working for Tingley, investigating him?"

"No."

"Did he phone you here about half an hour ago?"

"What?" Miss Bonner frowned. "Did who phone me?"

"Cliff. To tell you what to tell me?"

"He did not. You—you insufferable—"

"Save it. I'm sensitive. I don't want to hear it. Thank you very much, Miss Bonner."

Fox wheeled and tramped out. Apparently Miss Bonner was disinclined for any further association with him, for though he had to wait more than a minute for an elevator, since it was after six o'clock, she did not put in an appearance.

On the street again, he still did not return to where he had parked his car, but set out at a brisk pace, headed downtown. At 38th Street he turned west. When he reached Sixth Avenue he entered a drugstore and consulted a phone book, emerged and looked around, and crossed the avenue to the entrance of a building which had seen better days and would certainly soon suffer demolition now that the El was gone. After a look at the directory he took a creaky old elevator to the third floor, where a narrow hall led him to a door with a dirty glass panel which said "Womon" in the center, and in a corner said "Enter."

He entered.

Chapter 9

Piles of literature were stacked high in all available spaces of the medium-sized room which housed the administrative, editorial, business and distribution departments of Womon. The furniture—two desks, five chairs, a typewriter, a mimeograph, cabinets and shelves—was unassuming but adequate. Standing beside one of the desks was a worried-looking man, dipping bicarbonate of soda from a package and stirring it into a glass of water. Seated at the other, sticking stamps on envelopes, was a young woman whose plain tan woolen dress conformed to her curves, with a face that might have been thought attractive for customary purposes but for the formidable intellectual power suggested by the capacity of her brow. They looked at Fox and he said how do you do.

"Good evening," said the man. "Pardon me." He swallowed the mixture in the glass and made a face. "I eat too fast."

"Lots of people do." Fox smiled at him. "Nice place you have here. Compact."

"Nice? It's a dump. I used to have an office—" The man waved that away. "What can I do for you?"

Fox opened his mouth to start the approach to the query he had come to make, but the young woman got a word in first. She had finished stamping the envelopes and arisen to put on her coat and hat, and spoke to the man:

"What shall I do if the stuff from Wynkoop comes before you get here in the morning?"

"Take it and pay for it. I'll sign a blank check."

"Oh." She was getting her coat on. "I keep forgetting that Phil—I mean I can't get used to being rich. He's later than usual, but I suppose under the circumstances . . ."

Fox, instantly abandoning the modest minnow he had come for at this splash hinting at a bigger and better fish, transferred his smile to the young woman and barred her way to the door.

"I beg your pardon," he said, "but may I make a suggestion?" He pulled from his pocket the Womon Statement of the Basic Requirements of a World Economy. "A friend gave this to me, and I think it's fascinating, but I don't understand it very well. I want to ask some questions about it, but I'm hungry. You're just leaving and I suppose you eat, so why don't you eat with me and I can ask you the questions? My name is William Sherman."

"Good idea," the man declared. "She can answer more questions than the rest of us put together."

"I always read while I eat," said the young woman without enthusiasm, and in fact she had a heavy volume under her arm. She shrugged. "All right, come along."

"Here," said the man. "Application for membership in the Womon League. Take it with you."

Fox took it, and his dinner companion, to the Red Herring on 44th Street, having decided that there was less oxygen there than any other place he could think of. In the bar she accepted a cocktail as a matter of fact, and a second one with no special reluctance. After they had been conducted to a booth for two in the back room, it occurred to him that he didn't know her name, and he asked for it and got it: Grace Adams.

By the time they had finished with the mixed grill and were being served with salad, Fox was confronted with the fact that though his calculations had been sound, nevertheless his expectation had not been realized. The two cocktails, joined with the insufficiency of oxygen in the crowded and noisy room, and reinforced by a bottle of Burgundy of which she had tossed off her share without looking at it, had indeed loosened her tongue; but the looser it got the deeper she dived into the profound abstrusities of economic theory. She derided Keynes, pilloried Marx, excoriated Veblen, and consigned the gold standard to the crucible of hell. Unquestionably, Fox admitted, she got brilliant and even eloquent, but he was not buying a dinner at the Red Herring, which was expensive, for the sake of eloquence.

Patiently and obdurately and deviously, time and again he spoke of his eagerness to contribute substantially to the cause of Womon, but she ignored it and went on with her fireworks. He tried other subtle and crafty approaches to the subject of the Womon exchequer and its present condition permitting nonchalant drawing of checks to meet obligations on the dot, but either she didn't hear them or she evaded them with a devilish cunning, he couldn't tell which. By the time the coffee was served he was beginning to get a sinking feeling that he was doomed to utter defeat at the hands, or rather the tongue, of this female pyrotechnic geyser.

Then, lifting her demitasse, she spilled a little on the cloth and giggled, and Fox understood. She was simply soaring, and had been ever since the cocktails. He could have kicked himself. He looked her in the eye and demanded:

"About Phil's big contribution. How much was it?"

"Ten thousand dollars."

"When did he make it?"

"Today is—" She frowned in concentration.

"Wednesday," said Fox.

"Yes. Wednesday. Yesterday was—"

"Tuesday."

"Yes. Tuesday. Monday. He made it Monday."

"Was it a check, or cash?"

"Cash. It was all in—" She stopped abruptly. "Now wait a minute. Don't ask me about that."

"Why not?"

"Because you're not supposed to—I mean I'm not supposed to—"

"All right, forget it." Fox turned and caught an eye. "Waiter! My check, please."

It was in fact desirable that Miss Adams should forget it, so he tried to get her spouting again, but she was silent. She said nothing until, out on the sidewalk, he attempted to get her into a taxi and she refused point-blank. With her heavy volume under her arm, she marched off in the direction of Grand Central. Fox watched her for ten paces, then turned and made for Sixth Avenue.

But he didn't find Philip Tingley at the Womon office. The man who ate too fast was there, and two others fussing around with literature, but no Phil. Fox stated that he would like to meet Mr. Tingley because he had been informed by Miss Adams that Tingley could polish off his understanding of Womon, but was told that Tingley hadn't been there and nothing had been heard from him. Fox left, found a phone booth, called the residence of Arthur Tingley, deceased, and was told by the housekeeper that Philip Tingley wasn't there and she knew nothing of his whereabouts. He walked to 41st Street, maneuvered his car out of its niche, and drove to Nine-fourteen East 29th Street.

That dreary edifice was enough to convince anyone that a new world economy was needed there, even if nowhere else. Four flights up in the rear, Phil had said, and Fox climbed the smelly shaft, having found the vestibule door unlatched. The door in the rear on the fifth floor had no bell push, so he knocked, but got no response. After a couple of minutes he gave it up and returned to the street, sat in his car a moment considering alternatives, voted for home, and headed for the West Side Highway. At 10:20 he was winding along his private lane and crossing the little bridge he had built over the brook, toward the white house among trees on the knoll which was known in the neighboring countryside as The Zoo. In the house, he blew a kiss at Mrs. Trimble, asked Sam about the spraying, settled a bet for Pokorny and Al Crocker regarding the body temperature of a hibernating woodchuck, went to the cellar to see if Cassandra's kittens had opened their eyes, played guitar duets with Joe Sorrento for an hour, and went upstairs and to bed.

At 9:30 the next morning, Thursday, he was back in New York, in a phone booth in a barber shop on 42nd Street. He had already made four calls. To Nat Collins at his office: nothing new. To Amy Duncan at her apartment: the same. To the Tingley residence: the funeral would be at ten o'clock as scheduled, therefore Philip Tingley would not be available for conversation until afternoon. To the P. & B. Corporation: Mr. Cliff was in conference and could not be seen until later in the morning. Fox was now, his notebook open in his hand, talking to someone whom he had called Ray.

"I call that real service. All right, I'll hold the wire." He did so for a wait of several minutes. Finally, he spoke again, listened a while, and then said, "Let me call them back to make sure. GJ11, GJ22, GJ33, GJ44, GJ55, GJ66, GJ77, and GJ88 are all Guthrie Judd. Eight cars, huh? Must save him a lot of shoe leather. Much obliged, Ray. Come up and look at my new tractor some time."

He left the booth and shop, walked to the Grand Central subway station, and took an express to Wall Street.

The Metropolitan Trust Building was a microcosm, a fortress, a battlefield, a pirate's corvette—depending on the point of view. The building had forty elevators and the company had thirty-eight vice-presidents, almost a tie. Fox, however, was aiming even higher than the highest vice-president. He got out at the elevator's zenith and opened his attack on the Maginot Line that defended the approaches to his prey, his only artillery being a sealed envelope. Inside the envelope was one of his business cards on which he had written, "Urgent. Regarding Mr. Brown's visit to Mr. T. at ten o'clock Tuesday morning."

The difficulty was hitting the target with the envelope. A receptionist condescended to phone someone. A suave young man appeared and wanted the envelope but didn't get it, and vanished. An older and tougher man arrived and conducted Fox along a wide carpeted corridor to a room where a skinny middle-aged man sat at a desk with a stenographer on each side of him. To him Fox surrendered the envelope and he departed with it, the tough man standing by. In five minutes the skinny man reappeared, beckoned to Fox, and escorted him through a door, a room, and another door, into a spacious chamber of authentic, though a bit spectacular, elegance.

A man of threescore, seated stiff-backed behind an enormous flat-topped desk of amargoso wood with nothing on it but a newspaper, said, "All right, Aiken, thanks."

The skinny man went. Fox moved toward the desk. "Mr. Judd?"

"Yes." The voice struck Fox as a new and remarkable synthesis, an amalgam of silk and steel: "Tell me what you want, please."

Chapter 10

F ox claimed a tenth of the desk's area for his coat and hat, and a chair for himself. His accustomed smile was absent.

"Well," he said, "I'm a detective."

"I know who you are. What do you want?"

"I was going to on to say. A detective forms a lot of funny habits connected with his trade, like anyone else. For instance, when I parked my car in front of Tingley's Titbits Tuesday morning, a big Sackett town car was there at the curb, with a liveried chauffeur. I noticed its license number, GJ88, and upstairs in the anteroom a little later, when a well-dressed gentleman passed through on his way out, I jotted it down in my notebook. The next day, when my interest—and a lot of other people's—in Tingley's affairs had become acute on account of his death Tuesday evening, I was told that the tall well-dressed man who had called Tuesday morning was named Brown. There are so many Browns. I asked the Motor Vehicle Bureau which one has GJ88, and learned that this Brown must have been using a car which belongs to Guthrie Judd. I wished to ask you if he was doing so with your knowledge and consent, but seeing you, I recognize you as the man who called on Tingley Tuesday morning. Doubtless the secretary, and others there, would do the same. So now I would appreciate it if you will tell me what you talked about with Tingley when you went to see him day before yesterday under the name of Brown."

Aside from his eyes, Guthrie Judd's face betrayed no reaction whatever to that careful and lucid narrative. The gleam in his eyes was more steel than silk. He asked, with no change of tone, "What else do you want me to tell you?"

"That's all for now, but of course where it might lead—"

"It won't lead anywhere. Go out by that other door, please." Judd moved a finger to indicate it.

Fox didn't move. "I ask you to consider, Mr. Judd, that it will be more annoying to answer police questions about it than to tell me. Would you prefer to have me give my information to the police?"

"I would prefer not to be bothered about it at all." A faint curl of the lip might have been either irritation or derision. "Should the police ask a question I would of course answer it. Please leave by the other door?"

"You know a murder case is apt to get messy."

"Yes."

"You don't care about that?"

"Really, Mr. Fox—"

Fox got up, retrieved his coat and hat, and left by the other door as requested. As he waited in the corridor for the elevator, he muttered something unintelligible. In the alley called Wall Street, he sought the subway again, returned uptown to Grand Central, and emerged onto Park Avenue.

The atmosphere of the reception room of the administrative offices of the P. & B. Corporation was permeated with the spirit of the decade which developed the public relations counsel in his glory. The receptionist was really, though a shade remotely, receptive, with nothing in her manner to suggest that it was an infernal imposition to ask her to convey a message to Mr. Cliff: and the young man who showed Fox the way and opened the door for him was positively cheerful about it.

"Sit down," said Leonard Cliff. "I'm busy as the devil, but I will be all day, so—" He looked, in fact, harried and a little puffy. "I'm glad you came. I want to thank you for that business yesterday—the way you removed that—uh—misunderstanding Miss Duncan had."

"Don't mention it."

"Though I admit you made a monkey of me, calling me the way you did on my offering Collins a retainer—"

"You took it very well," Fox declared. "It's a good thing you don't mind being made a monkey of, because I came to do it again, and since you're busy and I am too, I won't prolong it. You were wrong about that OJ55. It wasn't OJ, it was GJ."

Cliff withdrew immediately, and in fairly good order. A flicker of his eye and a movement of his jaw, neither very pronounced, was the extent of his nerves' treachery. He sounded properly bewildered: "That must be a code I don't know. What are you talking about?"

Fox smiled at him. "Let's go at it another way. What newspaper did you work for?"

"None. I've never been on a paper."

"Then where did you learn how to write without beginning sentences with 'I'?"

"I wouldn't say I did learn how to write. But I wrote copy for Corliss & Jones for three years before I landed here."

"I knew you must have had practice." Fox looked pleased with himself. "Regarding that anonymous letter Nat Collins got yesterday—"

"What letter?"

"One he got. Let me expound. You're probably an excellent business executive, but you'd never make a good intriguer. When I asked you, there in Collins's office, where you were Tuesday evening, your glance at Miss Duncan and your change of color gave you dead away. Obviously, during those two and a half hours you were doing something for, to, at, by, or with, Miss Duncan, the recollection of which you found embarrassing. That, however, told me nothing specific. But you went out to the anteroom where Philip Tingley was waiting, and you knew it was he because you had heard his arrival announced. While he was in with us, Collins got a phone call saying that the man who entered Tingley's at 7:40 Tuesday evening was Philip Tingley. Since the anonymous informant had not known the identity of the man at the time he wrote the letter, he must have just discovered what Philip Tingley looked like. A little later I learned from Miss Larabee that you had been out for ten minutes at the time the phone call was received. So, as I say, I'm glad you don't mind being made a monkey of. My odds are fifty to one that you wrote the letter and made the phone call."

Cliff, composed, shook his head. "I hate to disappoint you, but it's a bad bet. A letter—a phone call about a man who entered Tingley's—it's all news to me—"

"Come, Mr. Cliff. It's a bad hand, throw it in."

"I know it's bad," Cliff admitted, "since I refuse to say where I was Tuesday evening. But I'm playing it."

"I implore you not to." Fox sounded earnest. "Tell me about it. It's more important than you know, and I guess I'll have to tell you why. You think you've given us all the information you have that would help us, but you haven't, because one detail of it is wrong. Your letter said that the registration number on the limousine was OJ55, but it couldn't have been, because no such number has been issued. What I want to know is how close you were to the limousine and how plainly you could see the license plate, and whether you might not have mistaken a C or a G for an O."

Cliff shook his head again. "I tell you, you're talking Greek—"

"All right, here's the point. There is a GJ55, and it belongs to Guthrie Judd."

Cliff looked startled. He straightened up and folded his arms. "The hell it does," he said quietly.

Fox nodded. "So you see."

"Yes. I see." Cliff screwed up his lips, staring reflectively at Fox's necktie.

"With most kinds of people," Fox continued, "a bold and bald statement of the fact would be enough. But in this case, I need to be sure of positive and immovable backing. If you can give it to me without an outrage on your optic nerve—"

"That part of it's all right. It might easily have been a G instead of an O, and since there is no OJ55 it must have been. It was dark and rainy, and I saw it from a distance as it drove off, and the light on the plate wasn't very good. I would be quite willing to state positively that it was G, at least for the purpose of pressure. But—" Cliff was silent, his eyes narrowed and his lips compressed, and finally shook his head. "But I can't do it." He shook his head again. "No, I simply can't do it."

"That's too bad. I got the impression that you were ready to go through fire and water, and maybe even splash around in the mud a little, to help Miss Duncan."

"I am. But it wouldn't be worth—after all, the main thing is the fact, and you have that—"

"Not enough. Not in this case." Fox leaned forward to appeal to him: "It might never be needed for anything but the pressure, and I'm working for Miss Duncan, and I want it and need it. Don't be so damn scared of a P. & B. vice-president getting his name in the paper."

"It's not that."

"What is it, then?"

"It's—" Cliff chopped it off, sat in uncertainty, and at length took a breath of resolution. "It's Miss Duncan. I was acting like a lovesick jackass."

"Well," Fox smiled, "evidently that's what you are, so what's wrong with that?"

Cliff's innermost concerns were much too deeply involved for him to return the smile. "I was watching her," he blurted. "I was following her."

"You followed her to Tingley's?"

"Yes. We had had an engagement for dinner and a show Tuesday evening, and she had canceled it. I thought maybe she had another—I couldn't help wanting to know what she did that evening. When I left the office—"

"Just after Tingley phoned you. Twenty to six."

"Yes. I went to Grove Street and watched the entrance to her apartment—that is, the building. I watched from across the street for nearly an hour, but when it started to rain I moved along to a doorway, and just as I did so she came out. She took a taxi at the corner and I managed to flag one soon enough to follow—"

"Wait a minute." Fox was frowning. "The rain."

"What's the matter with it?"

"According to you, it started raining around seven o'clock. Up at my house in the country it started around five, but that's sixty miles away, so that can't be what's wrong with it." Fox was scowling in concentration. "It's something else. There's some reason why it should have been raining long before seven o'clock right here in Manhattan. Are you sure it started at seven?"

"Certainly I am. Not more than two or three minutes before—"

"All right. Don't mind me, I have these spells. You followed Miss Duncan to Tingley's?"

Cliff nodded. "And wondered what in the name of heaven she was doing there, since I didn't know she was Tingley's niece. I dismissed my taxi. It was raining even harder than before, so I ducked into the opening of the driveway tunnel. You know the rest. When she came out—"

"What time was that?"

"Exactly eleven minutes past eight. I had just looked at my watch a moment before. When she stumbled and nearly fell I started toward her, but backed up into the tunnel again. Under the circumstances it would have been extremely embarrassing—anyway, I followed her to Eighth Avenue, wondering what could have happened to her, the way she was walking, wondering even if she was drunk—" Cliff halted, bit his lip, and shook his head. His voice shook a little: "If I had only known—but I didn't. She took a taxi and so did I. After she went into her apartment with the driver, and he came out again pretty soon, I stuck around over an hour, and at ten o'clock I left and went home."

Fox grunted. "If you had stayed ten minutes longer you'd have seen me arrive. Did you put everything that happened in that letter to Collins?"

"Yes."

"You didn't enter the building at all?"

"I just said that I put everything in the letter."

"Don't get touchy. I want all there is. Did you leave the tunnel at all between Miss Duncan's arrival and departure?"

"No. It was a cold rain and I had no umbrella or raincoat—only a cloth topcoat."

"You were there an hour. Could anyone have entered or left by that door without you seeing them?"

"No. I was thinking she might come out any minute, in spite of her having dismissed her taxi."

"How sure are you that the man in the raincoat was Philip Tingley?"

"Well—I told Collins on the phone, a hundred to one. When I saw him there in the anteroom—he has a very unusual face, but of course it was dark Tuesday evening and the street light wasn't very close. What decided me was his walk when he got up to go inside."

"I see. That'll probably do for him. But on the GJ55 you'll have to be prepared to get your back to the wall and show your teeth. And what about Judd himself? You saw him."

"The driver held an umbrella over him." Cliff hesitated. "It could have been Judd. When he came out he dived for the car and I didn't see his face at all."

"You saw him," Fox insisted. "For the—uh—pressure. You saw him."

Cliff considered. "I might," he agreed, "be willing to stretch a point for the pressure. But what if it goes beyond pressure?" He appealed with an upturned palm. "Don't misunderstand me, Mr. Fox. As unpleasant as it would be, I am prepared to be a witness at a murder trial if there's no decent way of avoiding it. This may sound sappy to you, but what I would dislike more—I mean, to have Miss Duncan know I was watching her and following her—"

"I thought you two were happily reunited."

"We are—that is—"

"Then don't worry. To have it known that you were tailing her to learn if you had a rival, and if so what he looked like, may make you ridiculous in the eyes of two billion people—roughly the population of the world—but not in hers. She'll think it's wonderful."

"Honestly—you think she will?"

Fox groaned. "And you an able, shrewd, cool-headed executive—you must be and you look it. It's amazing what can happen to a brain without impairing it in other respects." He glanced at his watch and got up. "But you're busy. I guess we understand each other. One thing, I am tentatively putting you in Miss Duncan's class and assuming that you did not go upstairs Tuesday evening and murder Arthur Tingley." He smiled. "Say ninety to one. But sometimes a long shot wins. I mention it only—"

He stopped because a buzz had caused Cliff to reach for his phone; and stood with the blank polite look one assumes when forced to listen to one end of a conversation which is none of one's business. From what he heard it appeared that Mr. Cliff's presence was being not only requested, but insisted upon, by someone strongly disinclined to take no for an answer;

and from the expression on Cliff's face as he pushed the phone back, it seemed that this new interference with his busy day was extremely unwelcome.

But the expression evidently was meant for Fox, and certainly the tone of voice was when Cliff spoke: "So," he said with biting contempt, "you give it to them first, and then come to appeal to me to help Miss Duncan!"

"It?" Fox's eyes opened in astonishment. "Them?"

"Yes, them. The police. Don't think you can make a monkey of me on this too. Inspector Damon wants me to call at headquarters immediately. He already has my signed statement covering everything he could want to ask about—unless you've told him about that letter and phone call and your damned deductions." Cliff set his jaw. "I'm denying it! You wanted it to help Miss Duncan, did you?"

"I did," said Fox quietly. "Quit going off half-cocked, or Damon will make a monkey of you too. Did he say specifically that he wanted—"

"He said nothing specific, but—"

"But you lunged for me anyhow. Steady up. You don't seem to realize that you're right plunk in the middle of a murder case in the borough of Manhattan, city of New York, you were at the scene when the crime was committed or darned close to it, and you have concealed that fact from the police—and also what you saw there. I didn't 'give it to them' before I came here, and for the present I don't intend to. I have no idea what Damon wants to ask you about, but he'll certainly keep on asking you things until this case is solved, and under the circumstances you'd better play them close to your chin." Fox had his coat and hat. "Good luck and watch your step."

He turned and went.

There were at least three things which required doing with as little delay as possible, and when, down on the street, he struck off in the direction of Grand Central and took to the subway again, he seemed to be aiming for one of them; but instead of emerging at Wall Street he stayed on the train for two more stations, got out and walked to Battery Place, and took an elevator to the top of the building numbered 17. The door he entered had painted on it: U.S. WEATHER BUREAU. He told a man with friendly eyes behind spectacles:

"I was going to phone for some information, but came instead, because I want to establish a fact beyond any attack by fire, flood or famine. What time did it begin raining, say in Greenwich Village, last Tuesday evening?"

He left ten minutes later, with the fact established as firmly as a fact well can be. The rain had started at 6:57. Up to that moment there had been no downfall, not even what is officially called a trace, in any part of Manhattan. The man with the friendly eyes had permitted Fox to scan the record and reports for himself. Fox, with a crease in his brow which betokened utter dissatisfaction with the state of things inside his skull, descended to the street, entered a Bar & Grill, and consumed four cheese sandwiches with lettuce and four cups of coffee like a man in a dream. The waiter, who liked to study faces, finally decided that this customer had just dropped his entire wad in a broker's office and was contemplating suicide, and would have been chagrined to know that in fact he was merely trying to remember what was wrong with the rain starting at 6:57 Tuesday evening. The crease was still on Fox's brow as he paid for his meal and left, took the Seventh Avenue subway to 14th, and walked to 320 Grove Street.

Mr. Olson, the janitor, was hanging around the vestibule. He watched Fox punch the button marked "Duncan" several times, but said nothing until he was addressed:

"Isn't Miss Duncan at home?"

"She may be and she may not be," said Mr. Olson. "If she is she ain't opening the door. There's been reporters and photographers and God knows what, trying all kinds of dodges to get in, and I'm staying here."

"Good for you. But you know I'm her friend."

"I know you was last night, but that don't mean you are today. She's in trouble."

"And I'm getting her out of it. Open the door and I'll—"

"No."

The refusal was so utterly adamant and uncompromising that Fox grinned at him. "Mr. Olson," he said, "unquestionably you are a good-hearted man, kind to your tenants, and well-disposed toward Miss Duncan. But I never heard a more unalterable 'No.' That had more behind it than a disinterested desire to defend beauty, youth and innocence from intrusion. What did Mr. Cliff give you, a twenty-dollar bill? Or even fifty? I'll bet it was fifty. You beat it upstairs in haste and tell Miss Duncan that Mr. Fox wants to see her." Fox's hand sought an inside breast pocket. "Or I'll serve you with a habeas corpus delicti and throw you in the coop."

Olson had courage, at that. "You stay here," he growled.

"I'll tend to me. Trot."

Olson went. In two minutes he returned, admitted

Fox, not too graciously, and stood at the foot of the
stairs watching him go up.

"The power of money," Fox told Amy when he
was in the living room and the door was closed, "is
enough to scare you. You might think you were Juliet
and Olson was the nurse. The P. & B. vice-president
bribed him. Did you go to the funeral?"

Amy nodded. She had on a simple dark woolen
dress and was without makeup, and her face was pal-
lid and strained. "I went to the services, but not to the
cemetery. It was awful—I mean the whole thing. It's
the first awful thing, really, that ever happened to me.
My mother's death was sadder, much sadder than
this, but not awful—she died so—so quietly. Yesterday a woman from the *Gazette* offered me three hundred dollars to let them take a picture of me lying on
the floor—unconscious like I was up there. And the
way—even there at the funeral this morning—" She
shivered.

"They have people with appetites to feed," said
Fox. "Not that I'd expect you to enjoy being an ingre-
dient of the feast." He stood, not removing his coat.
"Anything new from the forces of the law?"

"I'm to meet Mr. Collins at the district attorney's
office at four o'clock." Amy laughed shortly and self-
derisively. "And I thought I wanted to be a detective." Her hands twisted nervously in her lap. "I'm
getting—I guess I must be a coward. The way they
look and the questions they ask—and dashing across
sidewalks hiding my face—it would be all right if it
just made me mad, but I seem to get scared and my
knees get weak—"

"It's not very easy to take." Fox patted her on the
shoulder. "Especially when you started by getting
knocked on the head with a chunk of iron and opening

your eyes on the sight you did. Was your cousin Phil at the funeral?"

"Yes. That part of it was awful, too. All the faces, some of them people who had known my uncle all his life, and all just stiff and solemn—no real grief or sorrow, not a single one. Certainly he wasn't a lovable man, but when you're dead and the people who have known you best meet to bury you—" Amy gestured for the rest. "And right there, while they were putting the coffin in the hearse, Mr. Austin and Mr. Fry and Miss Yates came and asked me to go to some kind of a meeting at two o'clock—they're the trustees and they're going to sign papers and they wanted me there because they're afraid Phil may start a fracas and they thought I would be a restraining influence —"

"It's two o'clock now."

"I'm not going."

"Well, Phil doesn't throw bombs. Is the meeting at Tingley's?"

"Yes."

Fox frowned at her. "You're piling on the misery. To be under suspicion of murdering your uncle, and what goes with it, is naturally not very pleasant, but there's nothing revolting about the trustees holding a meeting immediately after the funeral. Quite the contrary. Arthur Tingley may be through with titbits, but those who remain aren't. You buck up and don't be morbid, and I'll kiss you again on your wedding day, one way or another." Fox took steps toward the door, then turned. "By the way, you told me that you got the phone call from your uncle a little before six Tuesday evening, and then you went to the bedroom and lay down for an hour. How did you know it was raining when you went to the bedroom? Look out the window?"

"I don't know. I suppose I did. Why, did I say it was raining?"

"You mentioned rain."

Amy looked uncertain. "But that was when I went outdoors. I don't remember . . ."

"You don't remember that it was raining when you went to the bedroom to lie down?"

"No, I don't, but of course if I said it—does it make any difference?"

"Probably not. Maybe you didn't say it—just an impression I got." Fox had the door open. "Don't get independent at the district attorney's office, follow Collins's instructions. For instance, don't mention that anonymous letter. We're saving it as a surprise."

Chapter 11

The ancient clock on the wall above the ancient roll-top desk said twenty-five minutes past two.

Since it was again the eight to four shift, the same two squad men were on duty as at the time of Fox's visit the preceding afternoon. The plump one was propped against a window sill with his back to the outdoors. The husky one was standing near the safe, gazing dourly at the occupants of the four chairs arranged in a square in the center of the room: Philip Tingley, Sol Fry, G. Yates, and a dapper little man with a bald head and a little gray mustache. This last —Charles R. Austin, attorney-at-law—was responsible for the gathering being located in that room in spite of everything. He had put his foot down. It was in that room that his senior partner, now long deceased, had formally read the will of Arthur Tingley's father thirty years previously, and it was therefore the only fitting place for the mournful ceremony which duty now compelled him to conduct. So that was where he was conducting it.

At this moment he was bouncing in his chair with resentment. He resented, certainly, the refusal of the policemen to withdraw decently from the scene; but what had started him bouncing a minute ago was the impertinent intrusion of an unannounced and unexpected visitor who had simply opened the door and walked in. Mr. Austin was sputtering:

"Nothing can excuse it! Good God, must you in your greed violate even the threshold of death? I tell you, Mr. Cliff, your generation which at the behest of financial masters and monsters has abandoned all scruples . . ."

The others let him go on. When he stopped for breath, Miss Yates looked at the intruder and said dryly, "You're here, so you might as well tell us what you came for."

Leonard Cliff, from beside Philip Tingley's chair, bowed to her. "Thank you, Miss Yates. I learned of this meeting—no matter how. You know that in behalf of my company I have been negotiating with Mr. Tingley for some time to buy this business. Ordinarily I would have waited, at least until after the day of the funeral, to resume the negotiations, but under the circumstances I felt that it was dangerous to wait at all. I have learned that Mr. Tingley suspected me of bribing his employees, or one of them, to adulterate his product, and I want to say that that suspicion was utterly unfounded. My company doesn't do that sort of thing, and certainly I don't. But I knew of the adulteration—"

Cliff stopped and turned his head at the sound of footsteps and the opening of the door. The others looked with him, making Tecumseh Fox the focus of seven pairs of eyes as he entered, took in the situation with a sharp glance as he approached, saluted the group with a nod, and spoke directly to Philip Tingley:

"I'm sorry, I guess I'm a little late."

The tactic was absurdly simple, but none the less

effective. To the policemen it established him as an expected addition to the meeting. To the three trustees it established him as expected by Phil, whom they did not desire to aggravate. And, as Fox had rightly concluded from the expression of cynical contempt on Phil's face, that young man was in no mood to challenge an interruption to a gathering which he obviously regarded as asinine.

"Excuse me," Fox murmured politely and self-effacingly. "Go ahead."

Eyes returned to Leonard Cliff. "I was saying," he resumed, "that I knew of the adulteration, and I had my own suspicions as to who was responsible for it, though I admit I had nothing to support them except my knowledge of the methods that have been pursued on other occasions by a man whose banking interests have recently gained control of a certain corporation. I knew that he wanted to buy the Tingley business. I have reasons to suppose that he was personally in touch with Tingley—uh—quite recently. I know that no considerations of propriety would deter him from any course he is determined to follow. I am aware that my appearance here at this moment is unseemly and you may even think it offensive, but I came to forestall the man I have spoken of."

"What man?" Austin, not mollified, demanded.

Cliff shook his head. "My description names him, or it doesn't. You people know as well as I do the honorable and enviable reputation of the Tingley business and product, started before any of us here was born. It would be a shame and a crime to let it get into the clutches of that man. My company offered Arthur Tingley three hundred thousand dollars for it. We want to buy it. We offer cash. I want to discuss it with you—if not now, then at your convenience, and before you make any other commitment. That's the request I came to make."

There was a moment's silence. Austin spoke: "All right, we've heard you. You'll hear from us when we have anything to say."

Sol Fry rumbled aggressively, "He can hear from me right now. I think it's a good proposition. This building is apt to cave in any minute, and for that matter so am I. I'm old and out of date, and I've got sense enough to know it." He glared meaningly at G. Yates.

Phil Tingley let out a hoot.

"We are a board, Mr. Fry," said Austin reprovingly. "We act as a board, not as individuals. But since you have spoken—have you anything to say, Miss Yates?"

"Yes." Miss Yates's soft and quiet soprano had yet a quality of unyielding determination. "I am resolutely opposed to the sale of the business to anyone whatever, at any price. I'll never consent to it this side of my grave. It was born here and it belongs here."

"I thought so." Austin compressed his lips. "That puts the whole thing up to me." He looked at Cliff. "Please draw up your proposal in triplicate and submit it to me as chairman of this board. I think you need fear no prior commitments."

"Thank you," Cliff said, and turned and marched out.

The plump detective shifted his position on the window sill, and the husky one, standing by the safe, yawned. Sol Fry and G. Yates regarded each other with open antagonism. Austin glanced inquiringly at Phil Tingley and then at Tecumseh Fox.

"I'm not trying to buy the business," Fox said reassuringly. He moved his eyes to embrace the group. "You folks probably have confidential matters to discuss, so if you'll just let me put a question—Miss Yates, what is your opinion of the likelihood that it was Philip Tingley who put the quinine in?"

Phil made a noise, stared up at him, and muttered in a tone of contemptuous disgust, "For God's sake." Charles R. Austin looked startled, Sol Fry incredulous, and Miss Yates imperturbable.

"I really want to know," Fox insisted mildly.

"Then ask me." Phil was sarcastic. "Sure I put it in. I injected it into the jars with a hypodermic needle I invented that goes through glass."

Fox ignored him. "May I have your opinion, Miss Yates?"

"I have no opinion." She spoke to his eyes. "As I told you on Tuesday, and as I have told the police, the quinine could have been introduced in the mixing vats, or on the filling bench, or later in individual jars. If in the vats, it must have been done by Mr. Fry, by one of the forewomen, Carrie Murphy or Edna Schultz, or by me. If on the filling bench, by one or more of the fillers. Philip Tingley had no access to the vats or the bench. But as I told you, it could have been done in the packing room downstairs by dumping the contents from the jars, stirring in the quinine, and filling the jars again. That wouldn't have been possible during working hours, but anyone with a key to either entrance of the building could have taken all night for it."

"Does Philip Tingley have a key?"

Phil growled, "I had a duplicate made at Tiffany's." He upraised his hands. "Here, search me. All I have at this place is a name that doesn't belong to me."

"I don't know," said Miss Yates. "Philip is Mr. Tingley's adopted son, and it wasn't my business to inquire what he had or didn't have, keys or anything else."

"It seems to me," Austin put in crisply, "that this inquiry, at this time and place, is impertinent and unnecessary. You are interrupting a meeting which, I may observe, is not open to the public—"

"I know I am." Fox smiled at him. "I apologize. What I really came for, I have been wanting all day to discuss a matter with Mr. Philip Tingley." His eyes moved to Phil. "It's private and fairly urgent, so as soon as you're through here—"

"I'm through now." Phil got to his feet. "Why they ever dragged me into this is more than I know. Come on down to the packing room and I'll show you how my needle works—"

"Philip!" Austin's voice trembled with indignation. "I have tried to control myself, but your conduct and your tone, in this very room where your father was murdered less than forty-eight hours ago—"

"He wasn't my father. You can go to hell." Phil tramped from the room and on out.

Fox followed him. The rooms were all empty, as Fox had discovered when entering. Apparently an item of the Tingley tradition had dictated the shutting down of the factory and office on funeral day, since there had been no cessation of activity on Tuesday afternoon, with the Tingley blood barely congealed. From a chair in the anteroom Phil got his coat and hat, then turned and surveyed Fox with no amity in the gleam of his deep-set eyes.

"Would you mind telling me," he inquired evenly, "the reason for the horseplay about my putting quinine in the damned titbits?"

"No particular reason. Just something to say." Fox looked around. "I did, and do, want to ask you something. Since there seems to be no one here to overhear—unless you'd rather go somewhere else—"

"Oh, no, I'm at home here. I own all this, you know. About as much as you own the White House. Go ahead and ask."

"I wondered if you'd care to tell me where you got the ten thousand dollars in cash that you contributed to Womon on Monday. Only three days ago."

The effect was considerable, but was in fact somewhat less than Fox had expected. Phil did not blanch or tremble, or even completely lose countenance, but the surprise of it made his mouth sag open, and his self-assurance abruptly retreated from his eyes to some inner line of defense.

"Ten thousand dollars is a lot of money," Fox declared. "I thought maybe someone gave it to you for injecting quinine into the jars with that needle you invented. That was really why I asked Miss Yates about it. I'm talking to give you a chance to collect yourself."

"I told them—they promised—" Phil faltered.

Fox nodded. "Don't hold it against them. I bought cocktails and wine for Miss Adams and she didn't even know she was telling me. Then there's another thing. About your passing out throwaways on 42nd Street Tuesday evening from seven to eight o'clock. I know a man—a veracious, intelligent and reputable person—who saw you enter this building at 7:40 Tuesday evening. You came out again in seven or eight minutes. You had on a raincoat and the brim of your hat was turned down. You came, walking in the rain, from the east, and went in the same direction when you left. Leaving, you were in a hurry—"

"It's a lie!" said Phil harshly. The self-assurance was gone from his eyes altogether.

"Don't talk so loud. Do you deny that you were in this building Tuesday evening?"

"Certainly I deny it! You're only trying—no one saw—how could anyone see me if I wasn't here?"

"You also deny that you had ten thousand dollars in cash on Monday. Do you?"

"I had—I'm not admitting—"

"It is presumably on record, entered as a deposit in the Womon checkbook. They know about it and I doubt if they would perjure themselves. Did you give it to them?"

"Yes." Phil's bony jaw was set. "I did."

"Did you get it from your father? Foster father?"

"No. Where I got it—"

"Did someone give it to you for putting quinine in the jars?"

"No. Where that money came from has nothing to do with quinine or this business or Arthur Tingley. And that's all I'm going to say about it."

"You refuse to say where you got it?"

"I do. You're damned right I do."

"What else are you going to say about coming here Tuesday evening?"

"Nothing. I wasn't here."

"Don't be a fathead. Of course you were here. You came to see Tingley and Guthrie Judd."

Phil stared, speechless, defenses gone, in helpless astonishment and consternation. The hoarse sound that came from him may or may not have been intended for a word. Then suddenly fierce anger blazed in his eyes and half choked him:

"It's him, by God! Him that says he saw me! But he didn't! He wasn't here! How could he—"

Phil's jaw closed as with the spring of a trap.

"Keep your voice down or one of those cops will be coming out to investigate," Fox said quietly. "Judd got here ten minutes before you did, and went away again before you arrived. I'm giving it to you straight because I can afford to. It wasn't Judd who saw you, it was someone else. Now tell me what you saw and did during the seven or eight minutes you were in here."

Phil's jaw stayed shut. His eyes, slits beneath his jutting brows, could scarcely be seen.

"You'll have to spill it sooner or later," said Fox patiently. "Here alone with me like this is as good a chance as you'll have. Did you come right upstairs?"

The pivot of Phil's jaw opened enough for him to get out, "I wasn't here," and closed again.

Fox shook his head. "You can't do that now. The mention of Judd's name got you. You're wide open."

"I wasn't here."

"You actually think you can stick in that hole?"

"I wasn't here. No one saw me. If anyone says he did, he's lying."

"All right." Fox shrugged. "Here it is in ABCs. Tingley was murdered and I'm working on it. So are the police, which is what they're paid for. By luck and wearing out my shoes I've made a little collection of facts which the police haven't got hold of. I can keep them for my private use up to a point, but beyond that point it would be not only risky but reprehensible. I ask you to tell me what you did here Tuesday evening, on the assumption that you did not murder Tingley. If you did murder him, you'll continue to deny that you were here, and soon, probably tomorrow, I'll feel obliged to hand my facts to the police, and they'll screw it out of you. Don't think they won't. If you didn't murder him, you're a fool if you don't come clean with me here and now. Let's start with the ten thousand dollars, since you admit you had it. Where did you get it?"

"It was mine."

"Where did you get it?"

"It was mine. I got it. I didn't steal it. That's all I'm going to say."

Fox looked at the stubborn bony jaw, the sullen obdurate mouth, the dogged expression of the eyes beneath the projecting brows.

"All right," he said incisively, "I'm not waiting till tomorrow. You and I are going together to one of two places right now. Either police headquarters or Guthrie Judd's office. Try balking on that and it will be a pleasure for me to take the necessary steps without any help. Which do you prefer, Centre Street or Wall Street? I think I should warn you that Inspector Damon, when he has something on you as he will have now, is a good deal tougher than you found him yesterday."

Phil was gazing at him. "You can't make me go anywhere with you if I don't want to."

"No?" Fox smiled. His right shoulder twitched. "A stupid mule like you? Damon wouldn't care what condition you were in as long as you could talk. And I'm pretty irritated." The shoulder twitched again. "Centre or Wall? Which?"

Phil swallowed "I have no—" He swallowed again. "I'm perfectly willing to go to Judd's office—"

"That's fine. Come on, and don't obey any sudden impulses."

Chapter 12

On this second visit the suave young man never appeared at all, in the reception room on the top floor of the Metropolitan Trust Building. Nor was Fox, entering, armed with a sealed envelope or any other weapon. He merely told the young woman at the desk that Mr. Fox and Mr. Philip Tingley wished to see Mr. Guthrie Judd. After a wait of five minutes the same tough man appeared and conducted them to the room occupied by the skinny middle-aged man, who now, instead of being flanked by stenographers, was confronted by three stacks of mail on his desk ready for signing. He asked what they wanted to see Mr. Judd about.

"I think the names will be enough," Fox told him. "Just give him the names, please."

The skinny man got up and went out. The tough man stayed. Before long the skinny man returned, but not alone. Entering immediately behind him were two individuals in uniform, male, sturdy and rugged-looking, with deadpans for faces. They came in three paces and stood. The skinny man spoke politely:

"Come with me, please, Mr. Tingley? Mr. Judd will see you first. You won't mind waiting, Mr. Fox?"

"It will save time if I go in with Mr. Tingley," Fox said, and moved determinedly to do that, but with the first step he knew he was licked. A man in uniform was on either side of the door, and he saw the mobilization of their muscles. To try to slug or shoot his way through would have been heroic but futile, and the setup made it plain that argument would be wasted. Gritting his teeth, he stood and watched Phil and the skinny man disappear. For a moment the impulse to dash to the nearest phone booth and call Inspector Damon was well-nigh irresistible, but he downed it because it would have been humiliating beyond endurance; and the advantage of surprise—surprise to Guthrie Judd at the sudden and unexpected confrontation—was lost anyhow.

Outwitted, euchred, defeated and deflated, Fox sat on the edge of a chair for thrity minutes, swallowing his saliva and finding it bitter with impotence and mortification. He had not even the consolation of seeing any smirk of triumph on the faces of the men in uniform: they remained deadpans. The skinny man had returned and was at his desk busily reading and signing letters. At a buzz he pulled the phone to him and spoke into it, or rather, listened to it, and then pushed it back and turned:

"Mr. Judd will see you now, Mr. Fox."

A uniformed man opened the door and Fox passed through; and the second door likewise. Guthrie Judd was seated at his desk of amargoso wood, erect, unsmiling and composed; Philip Tingley, in a chair near him, was tense in both posture and countenance and seemed uncertain whom to look at. As Fox entered with a guard at each elbow, not touching him but ready to, and approached the desk, Judd nodded curtly.

"Thanks, that will do. Leave us, please."

When the door had closed noiselessly behind them, Judd, otherwise motionless, moved his eyes to focus on Fox.

"So you came back." His voice was silk and steel as before, but with an edge to it, an edge that menaced as a sharp knife might menace a throat. "You're determined to make a nuisance of yourself, aren't you?"

"I am now, Mr. Judd." Fox met his gaze. "I'm good and sore. Not at you. I hope you're not congratulating yourself that you hung me out to dry, because I did that. If I hadn't been a moron I'd have kept your young friend in a bottle until I got in here. But I fumbled it, and now I'm sore; and when I'm sore—anyway, don't congratulate yourself."

A corner of Judd's lips faintly curled. "You will now, of course, go to the police."

"I don't think so. If I did that I'd have to describe my performance here, and they'd send me to an institution for mental defectives. So I guess I'll wait till I have more on the ball."

"Suit yourself." Judd's tone implied that it was no concern of his. "I asked Aiken to send you in in order to remove a misapprehension you seem to be under. I have never met Philip Tingley before. Have I, Mr. Tingley?"

"Certainly not," Phil muttered.

"But when his name came to me along with yours I naturally surmised that he was some relation of Arthur Tingley, and I wondered why he was here with you. The thing to do was to ask him, and I sent for him. What he tells me is astonishing, even fantastic. He says that you state that he had an appointment to meet me at his father's office Tuesday evening; that he went there at twenty minutes to eight for that

purpose and remained seven or eight minutes; and
that I had already been there, arriving ten minutes
before he did and leaving before he came. Further,
that I had paid him ten thousand dollars to adulterate
the Tingley product." Something resembling a smile
flitted over Judd's lips. "That last is even more pre-
posterous than the rest of it. I was poor when young,
I've made for myself what money and position I have,
and I assure you I didn't do it by paying large sums to
people for putting quinine into jars of food."

Fox nodded. "You can try that, but I doubt if it's
wise."

Judd's brows went up.

"I mean," Fox explained, "that even if I don't start
a fire under you and am compelled to give up, the
police are almost sure to flush you if you take that
cover. They'll work on Tingley here, and he's not
made of reinforced ice as you are. There's the man
who saw your car drive up at Tingley's at 7:30 Tuesday and saw you get out and enter the building.
There's the chauffeur who drove you there. There's
the ten thousand dollars, which came from somewhere. And the line you're taking is, 'Not me.' With
all your position and power, and the invincible will
back of your eyes, I doubt very much if you can carry
it off."

"Are you through?" Judd asked, with the edge
sharper on his voice.

"Thank you," said Fox.

"For what?"

"For a lead to a tag. I'm not through, I'm just
starting."

Fox turned and went, by the other door as previously.

The rush-hour crowd would be clogging the subway, but it was the quickest way uptown, so he took it, squeezing into a corner of the vestibule. On one side a girl's elbow dug into his hip, and on the other a man's newspaper tried to scratch his cheek, but he was oblivious. Swaying with the mass in response to the lurches of the train, his thoughts were all boomerangs, beginning and ending with the thorns of self-disesteem that were pricking him. At 42nd Street he fought his way out.

Since it was long past five o'clock there was a chance that he would be too late to catch Nat Collins at his office, but luck was with him. Miss Larabee was gone, but Collins was there, chewing gum and looking as if he would soon be in need of a shave, two invariable phenomena of the end of the afternoon. He greeted Fox and waved him to a chair and resumed chewing.

"News?" Fox demanded.

Collins shook his head. "Nothing explosive. Miss Duncan and I—what's this about your asking her about when it started to rain?"

"I got curious about it. File it. How was the D.A.?"

"So-so. It was Skinner himself. He covered about the same ground that Damon did yesterday, except that they've dug up some stuff about some unmarried mother there at the factory."

"That was years ago."

"Sure, but you know. The roots of crime are in the dark and hidden past. That was all right. We were only with him an hour, and I dropped in here and would have dropped out again if it hadn't been for a phone call. Do you know a woman at Tingley's named Murphy? Carrie Murphy?"

"Yes, one of the forewomen. Tingley trusted her."

"She phoned and wants to see me. Be here at six

o'clock. Probably had a dream last night and a big white bird sky-wrote the name of the murderer, and it just happens that it's someone she doesn't like."

"I suppose so," Fox agreed pessimistically. "I didn't have a dream, but it looks as if I have a pick between two for the murderer, and I've made an ungodly mess of it."

Collins stopped chewing and looked at him sharply. "Who are the two?"

"Philip Tingley and Guthrie Judd."

"Guthrie Judd? You're crazy."

"No, I'm only half-witted. But. The anonymous letter and the phone call were from Leonard Cliff. I've had a talk with him. As he said on the phone, the man in the raincoat who arrived at 7:40 was Phil Tingley. He was wrong about the OJ55, it was GJ55, and it belongs to Guthrie Judd. Therefore Judd was there at 7:30. Also he had been there in the morning, calling on Tingley under the name of Brown. I saw him."

The lawyer removed the gum from his mouth, wrapped it in a piece of paper and tossed it in the wastebasket, leaned back in his chair, and riveted his eyes on Fox.

"Go slower and let me look at the scenery."

Fox did so. Succinctly but in detail, he reviewed the day: the GJ55 in his notebook, the first assault on Guthrie Judd, the interview with Leonard Cliff, the meeting in Arthur Tingley's office, the talk with Phil in the anteroom, the second assault on Judd, the idiotic blunder he had been guilty of. Throughout Collins sat motionless and expressionless with head cocked a little sideways, a posture that was famous in New York courtrooms. When the recital ended he heaved a deep sigh and screwed up his lips.

"You couldn't have jumped them and made it through?" he asked wistfully.

"No, I couldn't." Fox was grim. "In the first place, they were a pair of pugs, and secondly, you're too busy to defend me on a charge of disorderly conduct, which is all I'd have got for my trouble." He pushed it away. "But forget that if you can, though I don't expect you to forgive it. It's the worst boner I ever pulled in my life."

"I admit it wasn't very brilliant. I also admit it looks as if one of them did it. Holy heaven and hell. Guthrie Judd?" Collins whistled. "That would be— what *that* would be. You've been chewing on it. What does it taste like?"

"Well—" Fox considered. "Judd hired Phil to dope the jars and paid ten thousand bucks. Tingley somehow discovered it, must have even got proof of it. That was why Judd went to see him Tuesday morning; he had to. It was also why Tingley had Phil come to his office at five Tuesday afternoon. He arranged for both of them to come back that evening at 7:30, and because he was desperate about Phil, to whom he had given his name, and because he thought his niece could influence Phil and perhaps contribute useful advice about him, he phoned her and asked her to come at seven, so he could discuss it with her before they arrived."

"But," Collins objected, "when she got there, at 7:10, Tingley was already dead, and the murderer heard her coming and hid behind the screen and knocked her on the head as she entered. So Judd didn't kill him at 7:30 and neither did Phil at 7:40."

"I am quite aware, " said Fox irritably, "that a man can die but once. And I am assuming provisionally that Tingley had already been killed, or at least had had his skull cracked, before Miss Duncan got there, for if not, it must have been he who laid for her and conked her. Which wouldn't fit anywhere, the way it stands now. In fact, I would say that we have to put it down that Tingley was already dead or unconscious when his niece arrived, or else reject her story altogether."

"I like her and I like her story," said the lawyer emphatically.

"So do I." Fox held up his fingers, crossed. "And the fact that Judd got there at 7:30 and Phil at 7:40 doesn't prove that one or both of them hadn't been there before. One or both could have arrived at any time between 6:15, when Miss Yates left, and seven o'clock, killed Tingley, started to search the room for whatever was wanted, been interrupted by Miss Duncan and knocked her out, got panicky and took a powder—"

"No soap. Cliff was watching in front and would have seen him or them leave."

"Not if they went out the delivery entrance. From where Cliff was—accepting his story—he couldn't see that."

"Judd wouldn't know about the delivery entrance."

"He might, but he probably wouldn't. But Phil would. He or they—I like it they—fled the scene without finding what they wanted, and went separate ways. Later each of them got up enough courage to go back for the object they sought, which was something small enough to be in the pocket of an overcoat, since Tingley's coat had been searched and left lying on the floor. Maybe one of them found it and maybe not. Also maybe, Tingley had only had his skull cracked, and it was 7:30 or 7:40, either by Judd or by Phil, that the throat-cutting was done when it was found that he was still breathing."

Collins grunted. There was a long silence. Fox chewed on his lower lip, and the lawyer stared at the process as if he expected elucidation from it. Finally Fox spoke.

"I'm giving myself," he said grimly, "twenty-four hours more. Until six tomorrow. Then I'll have to take it to Damon. Judging from my performance today, that's the best way to get Miss Duncan out of a jam, which is what I undertook to do—There's the fore-woman that's had a dream. Am I invited? Shall I bring her in?"

Collins said he would go, and went. In a minute he was back with the caller.

Carrie Murphy, in a brown coat with a muskrat collar, with a little brown felt hat perched on the top of her head, preceded the lawyer into the room with a determined step and a do-or-die expression on her face. She looked younger than she did in her working smock, as he stood appraising her while Collins helped in the disposal of her coat and pulled up a chair for her; and he decided that whatever she might have come for, it wasn't to tell of seeing a big white bird in a dream.

She sat down, directed a level gaze at the lawyer, and said, "I don't know much about lawyers and this kind of thing, but you're representing Amy Duncan and you must be the one for me to tell. Amy is in trouble about this, isn't she? I mean in the paper to-night—is she suspected of killing Tingley?"

"That's a strong way to put it," said Collins, "but —yes, she is certainly under suspicion."

"Well, she didn't do it. Didn't she get there soon after seven o'clock?"

"That's right. About ten minutes past seven."

"And wasn't she knocked unconscious as she entered the office?"

"That's right."

"And she didn't come to until after eight o'clock?"

"That's right."

"Then she couldn't have done it while she was unconscious, could she? Mr. Tingley was alive, talking on the telephone, at eight o'clock."

Chapter 13

ox's eyes went half shut and then opened again. Collins cocked his head and frowned.

The lawyer spoke: "That's a very—remarkable statement, Miss Murphy. I suppose you're sure of it?"

"I am," she declared firmly.

"Was it you Tingley talked to on the phone?"

"No. It was Miss Yates." She gulped, but her eyes were steady and her voice unfaltering. "I went to see her at her apartment Tuesday evening. We discussed something that made it—she had to call up Mr. Tingley, and she talked with him three or four minutes. She called him at his office. It was just a minute or two before eight when she rang off, because right after that a friend of hers came and I left and it was just past eight when I left."

"By your watch? Was it right?"

"I set it by the radio every day at six o'clock. Anyway, the time was mentioned, because Miss Harley—Miss Yates's friend—was expected at eight and she was right on time."

"Did you hear Miss Yates phoning Tingley?"

"Certainly. I was right there."

"Did you speak on the phone yourself?"

"No."

"But you're sure she was speaking to Tingley?"

"Of course. She was talking about—the business matter we had been discussing."

"What was that?"

"It—" Miss Murphy halted. She gulped again. "It was a confidential business matter. If I tell you I'll probably get fired. I may anyway. I spoke to Miss Yates about this yesterday, and said we ought to tell about it for Amy's sake, but she said it wasn't necessary, that Amy couldn't possibly be guilty and she'd get out of it all right. But when I read the paper this evening—I decided to tell you about the phone call. But that ought to be enough. I don't see that it matters what we were discussing."

"Did you often go to see Miss Yates at her home?"

"Oh, no, very seldom."

Collins leaned back and regarded her. "It's like this, Miss Murphy. If we pass this information on to the police, you can be sure they will insist, they'll demand, that you tell them what you were discussing with Miss Yates, because it was the subject of her conversation with Tingley on the phone, and they'll want that from her, every word of it. And unless you give us all the details I'm afraid we'll have to turn it over to the police, because we can't deal intelligently with information as fragmentary as that. I'm sorry, and I certainly don't want to get you into trouble, but that's the way it is."

She met his gaze. "If I tell you, Miss Yates will know I told you."

"Possibly not. She may tell us herself without our revealing that you have already done so. We'll try that."

"All right. I've started it and I'll finish it. It's a long story."

"We have all night."

"Oh, it won't take that long. Of course you know about the quinine."

"Yes."

"Well, for three weeks we've been investigating it. Questioning all the girls—everybody. And trying to prevent it's being done again. New locks were put on the storage rooms and packing room downstairs. Upstairs everything was watched every minute. Edna Schultz and I knew that Mr. Tingley had Miss Yates and Mr. Fry watching us, but they didn't know that he had us watching them. He called Edna and me into his office one day and said he didn't suspect us or Miss Yates and Mr. Fry, but that he had to act as if he suspected everybody, only he didn't want Miss Yates and Mr. Fry to know about it."

She was rattling it off, with the obvious desire to finish a disagreeable task as soon as possible. "Since this trouble began, the mixers and the filling benches have been watched every minute by one of us four. If Edna or I did a mix, either Miss Yates or Mr. Fry tasted it just before it was dumped into the trays going to the filling benches. They did that openly, and they also put some in a sample jar and labeled it with the mix number, and took it to Mr. Tingley for him to taste. But when Miss Yates or Mr. Fry did a mix, Edna or I took a sample without letting anyone see us, labeled it, and put it where Mr. Tingley could get it. He told us not to take it to his office because we almost never went there, and they would have been sure to notice it and ask about it."

Fox interposed, "Where did you put it?"

"I took it to the cloakroom and put it in the pocket

of my coat hanging there, and Mr. Tingley would go
there and get it. Edna did the same. It wasn't hard to
do it without being seen, since it was our job to dump
the mixers. But I guess I got careless, because Tuesday afternoon Mr. Fry caught me doing it and jumped
on me. He took me to the sauce room and commanded
me to tell him what I was up to, and Miss Yates came
in and he told her about it. She got mad at him and
told him that the girls, including Edna and me, were
in her department and she would handle it, and they
fought about that awhile until Mr. Fry got too mad to
talk and went out. Then Miss Yates asked me what
the idea was, and I was on a spot. I got flustered, and
when she got mad I did too, and I saw the only thing I
could do was tell Mr. Tingley about it. I bounced out
of the sauce room and up to the front, to the door of
the office. It was closed. I knocked, and his voice
yelled from inside that he was busy and couldn't be
disturbed."

"What time was that?"

"A little after five. About a quarter after."

Fox nodded. "He was conversing with his son.
Could you hear anything they said?"

"I didn't stay long enough. I went around through
the other offices and out the front entrance and on
home. But while I was eating supper I decided I had
acted like a fool. If I saw him and told him about it,
and he merely told Miss Yates that I had explained
the matter to him and she was to forget it, I would be
in bad with her forever, and after all she was my boss.
She had had a perfect right to demand an explanation,
since she didn't know what the real explanation was,
and I shouldn't have got my Irish up. I decided I
hadn't better wait till morning to fix it with her, so I
went to her place on 23rd Street and told her—"

"What time did you get there?"

"Right around half past seven. I told her the whole thing, how I had only been following Mr. Tingley's orders, and Edna too. At first she didn't believe me, I guess because she simply couldn't believe that anybody, Mr. Tingley or anyone else, could think she might be involved in that quinine business. She phoned to ask Edna about it, but Edna wasn't at home. She asked me a lot of questions, and finally she phoned Mr. Tingley, but found he hadn't come home yet, so she tried the office and got him there. When she rang off she was so mad she could hardly speak. She would probably have lit into me, though it wasn't my fault, but just then Miss Harley came and I got out. I thought she'd be cooled off by morning, but I knew I'd get the devil from Mr. Tingley for letting myself get caught. But in the morning . . ."

Miss Murphy fluttered a hand.

Nat Collins was frowning reflectively and rubbing his chin. Fox was regarding the tip of Miss Murphy's nose dubiously and pessimistically.

"Anyway," she said defiantly, "whatever happens to my job, Amy Duncan is a good scout and I won't have that on my conscience! I mean that I didn't tell about his being alive at eight o'clock."

Fox grunted. "It may help your conscience, but I'd be much obliged if you'd explain how it helps Miss Duncan."

"Why—of course it does! What I said—what you said—if she was unconscious—"

"She says she was unconscious," said Fox dryly. "Up to now I have believed her. I still would like to believe her. But if you're telling the truth—"

"I am telling the truth!"

"I admit it sounded like it. But if you'd like to see

Miss Duncan arrested for murder and held without bail, go and tell it to the police."

"If I—" She gawked at him. "My God, I don't want her arrested! The only reason I came to tell you—"

"Please!" Fox was peremptory. He rose to his feet. "I haven't got time to diagram it for you, but Mr. Collins will. You certainly have blown us sky-high. But before I start on a search for some of the pieces, please tell me: did the sample Mr. Fry caught you taking get delivered to Mr. Tingley?"

"But I don't understand—"

"Mr. Collins will explain after I go. Just answer my question. Did Tingley get that sample?"

"Yes. At least I put it in the cloakroom, in my coat pocket—that was about a quarter after four—and when I got my coat later it was gone."

"Were other samples delivered in that manner to Tingley on Tuesday afternoon?"

"Yes."

"How many?"

"Four or five." Miss Murphy considered. "I had— let's see—one Fry and two Yates, and Edna had two Fry—that was the two ham spreads—"

"All right." Fox got his hat and coat and turned to her again. "One thing. If you tell the police what you've told us, Miss Duncan will probably be charged with murder and thrown into jail. At least she'll be in great danger of it. Suit yourself. I hope you'll hold off for a day or two, but that's up to you. How do you feel about it?"

"Why, I—" Miss Murphy looked wholly bewildered and a little frightened. "I don't want—could they—I mean if I don't tell them and they find out about it, could they arrest me?"

"No," said Collins firmly and forcibly.

Fox smiled at her reassuringly. "He's a good lawyer, Miss Murphy. If you'll give me time to turn
around, say a couple of days, I'll appreciate it—
Where'll you be if I need you later, Nat?"

Collins told him the Churchill Theater and then
the Flamingo Club, and he left them.

As Fox walked north on Madison Avenue and
turned in to 41st Street, where he had garaged his car
that morning, no friend or associate who knew him
well would have been likely, after one glance at his
face, to stop him for a jovial word or two. Or even, for
that matter, to speak to him, since you don't speak to
a man who doesn't see you, and Fox wasn't seeing
anything or anyone. The attendant at the garage, seeing the extent of his customer's preoccupation with
inner affairs, trotted out to the sidewalk ahead of the
car to avoid a possible manslaughter of pedestrians.

But the feel of the steering wheel in his hands
automatically created in Fox's brain the appropriate
concentration of attention, excluding all others, as it
does with every good driver, and in spite of the emi-
nently unsatisfactory state of his mind, he arrived at
his destination on 23rd Street without scraping a
fender. The building he stopped in front of was certainly not modern but had an appearance of clinging
stubbornly to self-respect; the vestibule was clean,
with the brass fronts of the mail boxes polished and
shining, including the one which bore the name of
YATES, where Fox pressed the button; and the halls
and stairs inside were well-kept and well-lit. One
flight up Fox pressed a button again just as the door
was opened by Miss Yates herself.

"Oh," she said.

Fox said he was sorry to disturb her and asked if
he might come in, and was permitted, not graciously

perhaps but still not grumpily, to dispose of his coat
and hat on a rack in the foyer and enter a large and
comfortable room with a little too much furniture and
an air of being thoroughly contented with the status
quo. He accepted an invitation to a chair. Miss Yates
sat on an upholstered divan, on its edge as if it had
been a wooden bench, and said bluntly:

"In case you think you fooled somebody this afternoon, you're wrong. Arthur Tingley told me he didn't
trust you. Neither do I."

"Then we're even." Fox matched her bluntness.
"My trust in you is nothing to brag about. And apparently Tingley's trust in you was something less than
absolute, since he arranged secretly with Carrie and
Edna to check on you."

Miss Yates made a noise. The muscles of her face
tightened, but the expression that appeared in her
eyes could not have been called fear. Finally she began, "So Carrie—" and stopped.

Fox merely nodded.

"Very well." She wet her lips. "What about it?"

"Several things about it, Miss Yates. For one
thing, your extraordinary conduct. Is it true that you
spoke with Tingley on the telephone at eight o'clock
Tuesday evening?"

"Yes."

"Are you positive it was his voice?"

"Certainly I am. And what he said—it couldn't
have been anyone else."

"Then why—I don't ask why you didn't tell me,
since you weren't obliged to tell me anything if you
didn't feel like it—but did you tell the police?"

"No."

"Why not?"

She just looked at him.

"Why not?" Fox insisted. "You're intelligent enough to know that in their investigation of the murder that information was essential, vital. Did you want to obstruct the inquiry into the murder?"

Miss Yates's eyes were leveled at his. "You just said," she declared evenly, "that I wasn't obliged to tell you anything if I didn't feel like it. I'm not obliged to tell you anything now, either. But if I refuse to, I'm not fool enough to suppose that that will be the end of it, now that Carrie—" Her lips tightened, and in a moment she went on, "You asked if I wanted to obstruct the inquiry into the murder. I didn't care about that one way or another."

"You don't care whether the person who killed Tingley—knocked him on the head and cut his throat —is discovered or not?"

"Well—I care, yes. I don't suppose any normal person wants a murderer to go free. But I knew if I told about that phone call I'd have to tell what it was about, and I'm entitled to my pride, everybody is. There has only been one pride in my life—I've only had one thing to be proud about—my work. The work and the business I've given my life to—and for the last twenty years I've been responsible for its success. My friends and the people who know me, they know that—and what's more important, I know it. And when Carrie—when I learned that Tingley had actually suspected me, had actually had my subordinates spying on me—"

A flash gleamed in her eyes and vanished again. "I could have killed him myself. I could. I would have gone there if Cynthia Harley hadn't come—"

"But you didn't."

"No," she said bitterly, "I didn't."

"And you didn't tell about the phone call because

you didn't want it known that Tingley had you watched by your subordinates."

"Yes. And then later, there was another reason, when it came out about Amy's getting hit on the head and lying there unconscious for an hour. I didn't understand it, and I don't now, but I don't believe she killed her uncle or was involved in it, and I saw that if it became known that he was alive at eight o'clock it would make it a lot harder for her. So that was another reason. But not the main reason."

"But there was also," Fox suggested, "a pretty cogent reason why you should have told about the phone call. Wasn't there?"

"I don't know what."

"Your own position. As a murder suspect. You're aware, of course, that with the police you're still under suspicion. You have no alibi during the period that they now regard as the important one. It isn't very pleasant to be suspected of murder, and by telling about the phone call—"

Miss Yates snorted. "Let them suspect. Anyway, if they seriously suspect me of murder, what good would it do to tell them about the phone call? No one but me heard Arthur Tingley's voice, and couldn't they say I was lying?"

"I suppose they could." Fox eyed her gloomily. "I wish to inform you that at present it is not my intention to tell the police about this, and I don't think Carrie Murphy is going to, at least not right away. How about you?"

"Why should I tell them now if I haven't already? If they find out about it and come and ask me—and I don't trust Carrie or you either—"

"I don't blame you." Fox arose. "I don't trust myself after today. My heart's in the right place, but my brain's withering. Thank you very much. Don't get up."

But Miss Yates, adhering to the common courtesies even for a man she didn't trust, went to the foyer with him and let him out.

He got in his car and drove to Seventh Avenue and turned downtown. Near 18th Street he stopped in front of a restaurant, went in, and told the waitress to bring him something good to eat provided it wasn't codfish or cauliflower. He was not by any means indifferent to food, and even in his present deplorable condition would have become aware of it if he had been served with something inedible, but when he left half an hour later he could not possibly have told whether the contented feeling in his stomach should be credited to breast of guinea hen or baked beans.

The dashboard clock, which he kept set within a minute or two, said five minutes to eight as he rolled to the curb in front of 320 Grove Street, got out and crossed the sidewalk to the vestibule. A figure emerged from a shadowy corner and was revealed as Mr. Olson with a toothpick in his mouth. He announced that Miss Duncan's bell was still being ignored upstairs, let Fox in, and stood listening in the hall until voices from above assured him that this caller was still a friend.

Fox, however, saw plainly from the expression on Amy's face that though he might be regarded as a friend he certainly wasn't the right one. When the door opened he was confronted by a vision of youthful loveliness in a becoming green frock, eyes shining and cheeks a little flushed with warm though restrained expectancy; and the passage of the cloud of disappointment across her features was not swift enough to escape his glance.

"Only me," he said. "Sorry."

She tried to compensate. "Oh, I'm glad! How nice—I mean I was hoping you—here, let me have your coat—"

He let her put it on a hanger. A rapid swoop of his eyes showed that the room had recently received attention; the cushions on the sofa had been patted into shape and neatly arranged; the magazines and other objects on the table had been tidily disposed; the rugs showed no careless speck and the ashtrays were chaste.

"You going out?" he asked politely.

"Oh, no. Sit down. No, I'm not going out. I—will you have a cigarette?"

"Thanks. I suppose I should have phoned—"

He stopped, and she whirled, as a bell rang. "Excuse me," she said, and stepped to the door to the hall and opened it. Fox surmised, of course, who it was, and was inclined to look the other way not to constrain any display of sentiment that might be contemplated, but the sound of Amy's modestly effusive greeting tapering off on a note of bewildered surprise demanded his attention and got it. Whereupon his own brows were raised in surprise, for Leonard Cliff entered the room like a thundercloud, somber, grim and menacing.

Chapter 14

Fox, standing, said, "Hello there."

Cliff looked square at him and said nothing. Amy, having closed the door, came around Cliff and looked at him, with no shine in her eyes or flush on her cheeks.

"What," she faltered, "what has happened?"

"Nothing." Cliff bit the word off savagely. "Nothing much. If you two are talking business, I won't—"

"But Leonard—what's the matter?"

"I just came to ask if it's true that you're a detective working for Dol Bonner. That she assigned you to work on me. That your—my car hitting you was a fake. That the whole thing was a fake!" His voice pitched into harshness. "Well? Answer me!"

"My lord," Amy said in a very small voice.

He barked at her, "Answer me!"

"Really, Cliff," Fox intervened, "that's no way—"

It was a mistake in judgment, for Cliff had a more precarious grip on his self-control than his appearance indicated. With his teeth clenched in sudden ungovernable rage, he hauled off and started his fist for Fox's jaw. It met nothing but air. Fox ducked, side-stepped, collapsed like a folding stool, and was sitting

on the floor with his legs crossed. Cliff recovered his
balance and his stance and glared down at him:

"Get up! I didn't hit you! Get up!"

Fox shook his head. "Oh, no. That's the trick. You
can't hit me while I'm sitting on the floor, and if you
try kicking me, I warn you that my next trick won't
be so comical. If you'll take my advice—"

"I don't want your advice! I don't want—"

"Leonard!" Amy implored him. "This is so—so
foolish—"

"Is it?" He faced her grimly. "You're wrong. This
is where it stops being foolish! There's been a lot of
talk about making a monkey out of me. By that damn
clown. You didn't talk about it, you just did it! I ask
you! Didn't you? I ask you!"

"No, I didn't. I wouldn't ever—want to make a
monkey out of you—"

"No? I've asked you a question! Will you answer
it? Did you deliberately fake that meeting with me
because you were assigned to work on me? Inspector
Damon has told me you did. I've asked Dol Bonner
and she admits it. Now I—" His face worked and he
tried to arrange it. "Now I ask you! Did you?"

"Yes," Amy said. She was meeting his blazing
eyes. "That was a fake. But it stopped being a fake—
soon—even that very first time—"

"You're a liar!"

"I am not a liar, Leonard."

His jaw opened and he clamped it shut again. For
a fraction of a second the flame of anger and resentment in his eyes gave way to a weaker and more desperate gleam, a gleam of credulous hope; then that
was in turn replaced by dull despair and disbelief. "By
God, look at you," he said bitterly. "You're good. No

wonder you took me in! Right now you look as sweet and true and lovely—if I didn't know—"

It seemed that it was all over and that he could no further trust his strength to resist such blandishments even knowing they were false, for he turned abruptly and headed for the door. But after only three steps, just as Amy began a movement, he wheeled and faced her again.

"You expect me to believe it stopped being a fake," he said hoarsely. "God knows I'd like to. There's nothing in the world I'd like to believe as much as that! For hours I've been thinking about it, going over every minute, every little thing that happened. A week ago tonight, here in this room—do you remember— that was the most beautiful—"

"Yes, it was, Leonard."

"It was to me. What was it to you? A fake? I've gone back over every minute. That evening dancing at the Churchill—do you remember that? Or even the very first time, when we were driving around after dinner—that first time you let me touch your hand— the way you looked and the way I felt—right then you were suspecting me of being a crook and a damned scoundrel and working on me! You admit that was a fake! Then it all was! It is right now! What do you want out of me now? You're not getting paid to work me anymore. Why did you say I could come here tonight? Why don't you lay off and tell me to go to hell?"

"I don't want anything out of you—"

"Oh, yes, you do! You bungled your job and got suspected of murder, you lady detective, and you need my help—"

"No!" Amy's eyes snapped. "If you can think that—"

"Miss Duncan!" Fox, who had quietly transshipped from the floor to a comfortable chair, spoke sharply. "Don't make a brawl of it! The man's in pain, and you gave it to him. It may take a couple of sessions to remove all traces of doubt, but the least you can do now, in common decency, is to look him in the eye and tell him you are madly and hopelessly in love with him. Don't you realize the condition he's in? When he came and saw me here, he was so jealous he tried to sock me."

There were spots of color on Amy's cheeks. "After what he just accused me of," she declared with spirit, "I'm more apt to say I'm madly and hopelessly in love with you."

"No no. Climb down. You deserved more than you got. You were a lady detective and you were working on him. If I were in his place I wouldn't completely trust you until after the honeymoon."

"What—what I said—" Cliff, still hoarse, was stammering. "There is no—what I said—I don't believe—"

"You will," said Fox shortly. "If there was nothing worse than this to worry about, but there is. You spoke of Miss Duncan's being suspected of murder. She was, vaguely. But if two people tell the police what they've just told me, it won't be vague anymore. She'll probably be charged, locked up, and held without bail."

They stared at him.

Amy sat down on a corner of the sofa. "But—what could anyone—"

Cliff demanded, in an entirely new tone of voice, "What's this, a gag?"

"No. I don't make gags about charges of murder. I've seen a man electrocuted. Nor am I trying to make smoke without a fire, just to see if someone will choke—Miss Duncan, look at me, please, you can look at him later. I want to know what's wrong with your recital of what happened while you were in that building Tuesday evening."

Amy met his gaze. "There's nothing wrong with it," she said stoutly.

Fox grunted. "You said that you entered the building, went straight upstairs, turning on lights on the way, found the door of Tingley's office open, heard no voices or other sounds and saw no one, got to the edge of the screen and knew no more until you came to on the floor, got out as soon as you could navigate, and came straight here. Do you maintain that that's the truth and the whole truth?"

"I do."

"You're not going to change any of that this side of death?"

"I am not."

"All right. You, Mr. Cliff. I won't repeat your story, as you'll probably prefer to tell Miss Duncan about it yourself—"

"I doubt if she'll be interested—"

"Okay. You handle that part of it. What I want to know is, how much of it was true and how much wasn't."

"It was all true."

"You're sticking to that?"

"I certainly am."

"In spite of the statement I made a minute ago?"

"In spite of everything." Cliff was frowning uneasily. "But if Miss Duncan—I mean, I thought that was helping her—"

"So did I. And if you want to be gallant and lie to the police or a judge and jury to protect a lady detective, that's your affair, I have no objection. But understand this, you're an idiot if you lie to me. I want the truth."

"You have it. I resent—"

"Go ahead and resent." Fox arose and went for his hat and coat, returned, and included them both in a glance. "If you ask Nat Collins in the morning, he may tell you what happened today that puts Miss Duncan in real and imminent danger of being arrested for murder. I have stopped telling anyone anything. I still do not believe that either of you was involved in Tingley's death, but someone is lying for a world's record, and until I find out who it is I won't feel like talking. Good night."

Fox turned and strode out.

On the street in front, he sat in his car for twenty minutes with his arms folded, his head hanging, and his eyes closed. At the end of that time he jerked himself straight, muttered, "It's either that or let the cops do it," and started the engine.

But he didn't find Philip Tingley at the Womon office on Sixth Avenue. The result of his visit there was in fact entirely negative, for the man who ate too much was so unfriendly and uncommunicative that it needed no great perspicuity to guess that he and Miss Adams had been spoken to about divulging the identity of the ten-thousand-dollar contributor. But Phil wasn't there, so Fox left, sought a phone booth, called the Tingley residence and got another negative result, and drove to 914 East 29th Street.

The door in the vestibule of that dismal tenement was not unlatched as it had been before. Fox considered a moment, punched the first button in a row on the righthand side, and put his hand against the door, ready to push at the first click. When the click came he was inside like a flash and on his way up the dimly lighted stairs. Just short of the first landing he halted, waited till he heard a door open below, called down, "Thanks very much, forgot my key!" and resumed the ascent. Four flights up, he knocked on the door in the rear, stood hoping for the favor of one little break, and got it. Steps sounded from within and he got his weight ready to oppose reluctance, but that wasn't necessary. The door swung wide and Philip Tingley was there. He scowled when he saw who it was, and without a word started the door on a return journey, but it was obstructed by Fox's hundred and seventy pounds after only ten degrees of its arc.

"Get out!" Phil demanded sullenly. "You can't pull any rough stuff with me!"

Fox, resolved not to commit another costly blunder in his relations with this six-foot bony eel, refrained from pushing past him for fear he might make a dash for the stairs and the street. Instead, he pushed against him, crowding him back to make room for closing the door; and got a surprise when Phil suddenly and astonishingly displayed capabilities as a man of action. Long arms shot out and long bony fingers gripped Fox's throat, and the grip was anything but puny. Fox went for the wrists and got them, but to his amazement they were immovable; he was gagging and choking and the muscles of his neck were helpless; a terrific stifling pain was in his constricted gullet and his eyes were going to pop out. He abandoned the wrists, hooked his right elbow, and crashed his fist against Phil's jaw, but the blow was glancing and lost most of its force through the interference of Phil's biceps. Fox hooked again, this time cutting up from beneath between the two arms, straight for the button, and that did it. Phil's head snapped up with a noise like a spasmodic snore, his grip loosened, and he staggered back.

Fox moved his own head slowly from side to side and tried swallowing. In a moment, when he was sure the road was open for words, he would instruct Phil not to be foolish. But that didn't get done, for before he could speak Phil came at him again, not trying for his throat this time, but apparently intending to break through the open door. He came fast, but Fox was faster. He stopped him with his left, clipped him with his right, and Phil toppled to the floor. As he went down Fox whirled and swung the door shut all but two inches, applied his ear to the crack, and listened. No sound of steps or voices came, so he softly closed the door till the lock snapped to, and turned just as Phil was lifting himself to his elbow.

"Look," Fox said, "I don't want to bust any more knuckles—"

Phil opened his mouth and started a bellow that promised to send waves all the way to Centre Street.

Fox leaped for him. Before the bellow swelled into full volume, he got a hold on his throat, with his thumbs in position to choke off utterance without doing serious damage, but it was immediately evident that that would not do. Phil struggled, writhed, clawed, banged the floor with his heels. Fox, tightening the grip on the throat with his left hand, doubled his right fist and planted it accurately and scientifically on the mandible hinge. The clawing and banging stopped.

Fox frowned at his right hand, opening and shutting the fingers, looked at the motionless figure on the floor and muttered, "The stubborn son-of-a-gun," and resumed activity. Rapidly he made a survey of the place, and found nothing in the nondescript furnishings of the two small rooms and smaller kitchen that was sturdy enough to withstand any violent effort at displacement, except the water pipes. Luckily, the kitchen cupboard yielded a length of clothesline, and the bathroom cabinet a roll of adhesive tape. A glance without showed him that Phil was stirring, so he lost no time. The tape, properly and plentifully applied to the mouth, precluded another bellow, and two pieces of clothesline secured the wrists and the ankles. Another piece of line lashed a wooden chair firmly to the water pipe in the kitchen, and still others, after Phil had been dragged in there and seated in the chair, fastened down his shoulders and thighs and all but immobilized him.

Fox looked the job over, nodded with satisfaction, got a drink of water from the faucet, brought another chair from the bedroom and sat on it, lit a cigarette, and regarded his captive.

"Well, here we are." He took another puff. "I did you up like that because there's no telling how long this will last and I'll probably want to go out for meals and exercise. At intervals I'll remove enough tape for you to articulate, and when I do so I hope you won't compel me to any more violence, because I only enjoy it when it's tough going. My minimum demands are these: Tell me where you got that ten thousand dollars and what for, and tell me what you did and what and whom you saw in the Tingley building Tuesday evening. After I get that we'll understand each other better and we'll see."

He took another puff, went and put out the cigarette in a saucer on the table, and returned to his chair. "I'll try to be patient and placid, but I'm apt to get impetuous when things go wrong, and they've never gone any wronger. To be forced to resort to this sort of thing hurts me worse than it does you, and that's not a joke. And I know it won't get me anywhere if you murdered Tingley, because you have a certain amount of guts, but if you didn't murder him this will get results and don't think it won't. You won't be the same man in seven or eight hours that you are now. I have in mind a little mechanical arrangement that will keep you awake while I take a nap. By the time I come back from breakfast—"

A bell was ringing, there in the kitchen. Fox jerked around, and was on his feet. Since there was no bell from the hall door, it must be from the vestibule downstairs. He found the button, above the sink, and punched it, observing as he did so that the muscles of Phil's arms and legs were swelling and twisting and his eyes were glaring in helpless fury. Fox took a swift look at the knots, stepped outside, closed the kitchen door, and opened the door to the public hall. He listened. The footsteps coming up the stairs were faint, light, lagging; there was a long pause, presumably for the collection of breath; then they were resumed. Before a head appeared at the rim of the landing Fox had decided definitely that it was a woman and quickly considered his line for a Murphy or Yates or Adams or Duncan. But it was none of those, though it was a female. Achieving the landing, panting, and glancing uncertainly toward the front before she caught sight of Fox standing in the doorway at the rear, he had a chance to appraise her. She was over fifty, was slim and well-preserved and stiffly handsome, and looked furtive and frightened; and the mink coat she was wearing had cost enough to pay the rent for all the apartments in that tenement for a year.

Fox took a step into the hall. "How do you do."

"Oh!" It was a little gasp from her. She moved toward him and stopped again. "Oh!" She came two more short steps. "You—are you Philip Tingley?"

Fox nodded and smiled at her. "This is me at the entrance of my castle."

"I'm late," she said inconsequently. She came closer and he got, faintly, her perfume. "I'm always late." She looked nervously around. "Let's go inside."

He stepped aside, entered behind her, and closed the door. As he motioned her to the farther room, her head jerked around at a sound from the kitchen, but he reassured her: "Just my dog. I shut him in there because he jumps on people." He followed her within. "Let me take your coat. This isn't the sort of chair you're used to, but it'll have to do."

She glanced around and he saw a shudder of repugnance run over her; and she permitted just enough of her person to touch the shabby soiled upholstery to call it sitting. Then he saw, by the intentness of her eyes as they fastened on him, that there was something about him sufficiently interesting or compelling to make her ignore the surroundings after that first involuntary spasm of fastidious distaste. He sat. She did not, apparently, intend to speak, and the fixity of her gaze made him wary; it seemed likely he was supposed to say something cogent and to some purpose, and therefore it was risky to say anything. But if she was determined merely to sit and stare at him. . . .

He smiled at her and asked pleasantly, "Do I fall short of expectations? I mean, the way you look. . . ."

She stiffened. "Nothing like that is in my mind,"

she said coldly. "Understand that. I had no—expectations. I came here only because your impossible conduct, your impossible demands, compelled me to come to appeal to you to have some regard for decency. I expect and desire no filial sentiments from you."

Chapter 15

Fox permitted himself three seconds for a rapid movement and reorganization of his cerebral forces, covering the operation by wiping his face with his handkerchief.

"Wrestling with the dog made me sweat," he observed.

The lady in mink had nothing to say to that.

"Naturally," he went on, "I disagree with your characterization of my conduct and demands." Smiling pleasantly at her had of course been wrong, and he was meeting her intent regard with a rude stare. "And I certainly have no intention of making any display of filial sentiment, even if I felt any, which I don't. If you're going to appeal to me . . ." He left it hanging.

She continued to gaze at him another moment and then said abruptly, "My brother told me you were a blackguard. A vulgar common swindler. I think he made a mistake." A frosty smile was on her lips and gone. "A woman can tell those things better than a man. You don't look—that way. My brother is not very tolerant or understanding, and I think he handled—undoubtedly he was blunt about it." She tried

to smile again. "That's his manner. He probably in-
sulted you about this—this business you want the
money for—"

"Womon," said Fox aggressively.

She nodded. "Whatever it is. He thinks that's just
a sham and a pretense, that you really want the
money for yourself. He doesn't realize, as I do, that
young people are often genuinely unselfish and idealistic. But a million dollars—that's impossible! He
won't pay it!"

"I think he will," said Fox menacingly.

"But he won't!" She extended a gloved hand, and
let it fall again. "I admit that I would, if I had it, but I
haven't. I have nothing. I have come here, to this
place, to appeal to you! I am dependent on my brother
for everything. He has been generous with me, but I
am dependent on him, and to expect him to pay any
such sum—even half that—"

"He will. He'll have to." Fox scowled at her. "You
might as well cut it. If all you came for is to try to
save him some money, you may as well save your
breath. You know damn well he'll pay it."

She was silent, gazing at him. Her jaw twitched,
and her lips worked, but Fox was saved the bother of
swallowing any compunction by the expression of her
eyes, for even in fear and real distress there was no
softness in them. He had no difficulty to maintain his
scowl intact.

"You are a blackguard," she said in a thin hard
tone. "You are willing to ruin me. I bore you, and you
would destroy me. Then this is what I want to say.
You think my brother will pay what you demand.
Maybe he will. I don't know. But I know he won't on
your terms. He has already given you ten thousand
dollars. He won't give you another cent, this I know,

until you give up the papers about—your birth—and
until you sign what he wants you to about that, and
about your going to meet him that evening. If you do
tomorrow what you threatened to do if you don't get
the money, you'll lose everything and so will I. That's
what I came to tell you, that's why I was willing to
suffer this intolerable humiliation, because apparently
you think my brother is bluffing, and he isn't. I know
him."

"I am not bluffing either—uh—madam."

"I suppose you're not." Deep and bitter resentment was in her eyes and tone. "You're a man—look
at you! I was doomed to be ruined by men. When I
was a poor little pretty thing in that factory—that
finished me, I thought, with men—but there are more
ways than one. You have some of me in you, and my
blood is the same as my brother's. Your father—you
haven't learned from those papers who your father
was, have you?"

"No."

"He was hard, too, in a different way from us. But
you're half him and half me." She laughed, a terrible
little puff of rancor. "So I wouldn't expect you to bluff.
But I have warned my brother and I came here to
warn you: unless you fix this, unless you two somehow
make terms, all of us will suffer. I'll be smashed, finished. His pride will get a blow that it will never re-
cover from, hard as he is. You won't get a dollar, let
alone a million. And there's another thing."

"Still another?"

"Yes." Her eyes bored into his. "Tuesday night."

"What about Tuesday night?"

"Don't be inane," she said contemptuously. "I
don't know who killed Arthur Tingley. Do you? Does
my brother? I don't know."

"Same here," said Fox gruffly. "That's no good with me for an inducement to compromise. But you knew we were going to be there, and I've been wondering if you didn't decide to make the gathering complete—"

The gleam of disdain in her eyes met the sentence and stopped it.

"All right." He shrugged. "Then let us worry about who killed Tingley, if you're out of it. As for the rest—shall I tell you what I think?"

"I came here in the hope that you would prove to be capable of thought."

"I am. I hope he is. I've been going over it, and I've come to the same conclusion you have. If we don't look out nobody will win and everybody will lose. But he's a hard man to deal with, you know that. I think if you were with us, if the three of us were together, we would get somewhere. I think the thing to do is for you and me to go to him now and settle it."

She frowned. "But he—" She seemed to be shrinking. "He would be—"

"You're afraid of him." Fox was on his feet. "I don't blame you, but you are. I'm not. I've got him where I want him, and you too. Suit yourself. I'm ready to go."

She shivered a little.

"Where is he, at home?" Fox asked.

"Yes. Waiting for me . . ."

"Suit yourself. If you want it settled—I don't know how I'll feel about it tomorrow—"

"Wait a minute." Her head drooped, and for a while she sat there motionless, her face not visible to him. Then she straightened up, arose, and said in a controlled voice, "Very well. We'll settle it."

Fox lost no time getting her out of there. But out in the public hall, before he closed the door, he turned to her as one who has suddenly remembered something:

"The dog. I'd better give the dog a bone. I'll be right back."

He slipped away and into the kitchen. A quick inspection of the bonds of the captive showed that all the knots were still intact, which might have been expected, since that had been his intention when he tied them. To the eyes that blazed with fury he paid no attention whatever, as he applied two more strips of tape to the mouth, and then began exploring pockets, not finding the bunch of keys until he got to the right hip of the trousers, which was hard to get at. Back at the entrance door, he would have liked to make sure the right key was there for his re-entry, whenever that might be, but the lady in mink was standing waiting, facing him, so he merely pulled the door shut for the spring lock to catch.

She preceded him down the four flights, and from the way she steadied herself with her fingertips along the grimy old rail it was plain that those gloves would have a cleaning before they were worn again. Outside, there was no car in front but his own, and he decided to ignore that, since he wished to preserve appearances and it was an unlikely chattel for an idealistic young man who lived in squalor.

He hesitated. "Your car?"

"I didn't bring it. I didn't want to—I came in a cab."

He turned west and they walked together to Second Avenue and after a short wait flagged a passing taxi, and she gave an address in the Seventies just east of Fifth. She took her corner and he took his, and nothing was said until the destination was reached, the driver was paid, and he hopped out and offered her a hand which she did not take.

There on the sidewalk, she looked smaller, less erect, her eyes less determined and hard.

"I had better go in first," she said, "and tell him—"

"No," Fox said bluntly. "We're doing this together or not at all."

She didn't insist. Fox depressed the lever of the massive ornamental door to the vestibule, pushed, held it for her to enter, and followed. She touched a button in the jamb, and almost at once the inner door opened and she passed through, with him at her heels. A man in the conventional uniform closed the door and stood ready for anything from negation of his existence to decapitation without change of expression.

"Is Mr. Judd upstairs?"

"Yes, Miss Judd."

"Then just take my things here." He was behind her for her coat. "And take Mr.—"

"Sherman," Fox said.

"Of course. Mr. Sherman's coat and hat."

That was done. Fox followed her across the spacious reception hall and up the broad carpeted stairs, admiring the fine old cherrywood of the curving rail and comparing it with the rail she had touched so gingerly less than half an hour ago. Upstairs was a landing only less spacious than the hall below, and broad corridors in three directions. She led the way to the right, opened a door, and passed through, into a large room of warmth and color and comfort and a thousand books. Only one person was there, a man in an easy chair with his feet raised to a stool, smoking a pipe and reading a magazine. His head turned to them as they entered.

Miss Judd spoke in a high-pitched voice. "Guthrie, I thought the best thing—"

She stopped and stood transfixed, at the expression on her brother's face.

Chapter 16

Fox said, in a tone of malign and insufferable affability, "I've got that fire started, Mr. Judd." To say that, in that tone, required an exceptional degree of tough audacity. It was doubtful if ever before, in all his ruthless, cold-blooded, predaceous career, Guthrie Judd had been rendered incapable of speech by a paroxysm of helpless rage, and to watch it happening on his face might have been found momentarily terrifying by almost anyone. The cold fury of his eyes, in particular, made credible the fable of the basilisk; but Fox, standing with his hands in his coat pockets and his legs apart, was meeting them.

Miss Judd was not. "I thought—" she faltered. "It seemed best—" She couldn't go on.

"She had never seen him," Fox said brusquely. "I was there, and she took me for him. We have discussed it fairly completely. Now I'd like to discuss it with you."

"She—took you for Philip Tingley?"

"Yes. That's why she brought me here."

Judd looked at his sister and said in a tone of caged and concentrated ferocity, "Get out."

She was gaping at Fox. "You—" The rest was stifled in pale incredulity. "You said—then who—"

"Get out!" Judd moved toward her, one step. "Get
out now! You incomparable fool."

Her mouth opened again, but nothing came out of
it. She was now perforce meeting her brother's eyes,
and plainly had no will against them.

He said, "Go to your room and stay there. I may
send for you."

She turned and went, walking like an automaton.
Fox opened the door for her, and after she had passed
through closed it again, returned to the middle of the
room, and said composedly:

"This is a very satisfactory moment for me. Very.
The two other times I called on you, you were so un-
sociable that it wasn't worthwhile to sit down. Maybe
I'd better take a chair this time?"

Guthrie Judd, without saying anything, picked up
his magazine, which had dropped to the floor, and put
it on a table. With his foot he pushed the stool to one
side. He sat down, got a lighter from his jacket
pocket, flicked it into flame, lit his pipe, and took several puffs. Then he said:

"Sit down."

Fox pulled a chair to a more frontal position and
sat. He waited through some seconds of silence and
finally asked, "Well?"

Judd shook his head. "Oh, no. I'm listening to you."

Fox shrugged. "All right. Philip is your sister's
illegitimate son. There are documents to prove it."

"Show them to me."

Fox smiled. "You certainly have good rubber in
you. Tough as catgut. But it won't do you any good
now, because you're on your back. You're licked."

"I have never been licked."

"Are you now?"

"No."

"Then this is your house. Order me out. You certainly didn't invite me to sit down for conviviality. Order me out."

Judd said nothing.

"You see," Fox admonished him. "You might as well quit taking me for a lightweight. Asking me to show you the documents! I may be no blazing luminary, but I am not a lightweight. I am quite aware that you are a dangerous man to monkey with, and if I had my per capita share of prudence I would take the bag just as it is down to headquarters and let Inspector Damon open it. Today you sneeringly invited me to do that. Do you now?"

Judd said nothing. His pipe had gone out again.

"You don't. Indeed you don't." Fox got notebook and pencil from his pockets. "Now. When did Philip first demand money from you under a threat to publish his parentage?"

Judd shook his head. He spoke, but all he said was, "I've looked you up. I can find no—"

Fox laughed. "Let me save you some trouble. You're going to say that you can find nothing in my past to support a supposition that I'm addicted to blackmailing. But money is money. You wouldn't insult me by trying to buy me, but you will pay a legitimate sum for legitimate services, like for instance getting those papers for you. And for helping—"

"One hundred thousand dollars," said Judd curtly.

"Nope. I would come even higher than Philip, and he's asking for a million. I'm in this thing because I got my generosity appealed to, I got my curiosity aroused, and I got my pride hurt. Didn't I tell you I was sore? I'm not interested in your family affairs as such, and no amount of money would make me interested. I am going to find out who killed Arthur Tingley. You and Philip had an appointment to meet at his office Tuesday evening, and you both went there. I know that a man like you will tell this kind of thing only under a compulsion that can't be faced down or ignored or smashed or wiggled through. You're under that compulsion right now. Either you give it to me, all of it, or Damon and the district attorney will be here within an hour. And we'll start at the beginning, with a few test questions. Remember I've had a talk with your sister. Who was Philip's father?"

Judd, moving with deliberate slowness, knocked the ashes from his pipe into a tray on the table, filled it again from a pouch he fished out of his pocket, applied the lighter, and got it going well. It was through a gray-blue cloud that he finally spoke:

"You are intelligent enough, I suppose, to have considered all the possible consequences—to you, I mean—of what you're doing?"

"Sure. Don't let that worry you."

"Very well. Philip's father was Thomas Tingley, the father of Arthur Tingley."

To cover the faulty control which permitted an involuntary start of surprise at this remarkable news, Fox coughed and got out his handkerchief. "So," he said, "Arthur was Philip's brother."

"Half brother." Judd's face and voice were completely expressionless. "Thomas was married and had two children, a son and daughter, by his wife. The son was Arthur."

"Was the wife still alive when—"

"Yes. My sister went to work in the Tingley factory in 1909. I was then twenty-five years old, just getting started. She was nineteen. Arthur was a year or two younger than me. His father, Thomas, was approaching fifty. In 1911 my sister told me of her difficulty and who was responsible for it. I was making more money then, and I sent her to a place in the country. In September of that year the boy was born. My sister hated him without ever seeing him. She refused to look at him. He was placed in a charity home, and was forgotten by her and by me. At that time I was occupied with my own affairs to the exclusion of considerations that should have received my attention. Years later it occurred to me that there might be records at that place which would be better destroyed, and I had inquiries made."

"When was that?"

"Only three years ago. I learned then what had happened. Thomas Tingley had died in 1913, and his wife a year later. Arthur had married in 1912, and his wife had died in childbirth in 1914, and the child had died too. And in 1915 Arthur had legally adopted the four-year-old boy from the charity home."

"You're sure it was that boy?"

"Yes. I went to see Arthur. He knew the boy was his half brother. His father, on his deathbed, had told him all about it and charged him with the child's welfare—secretly, since at that time Thomas's wife was still alive. Two years later, after Arthur's wife had died and he was childless, he had decided on the adoption."

Fox, from scribbling in his notebook, looked up. "When you saw Arthur, three years ago, did he have the records you wanted?"

"Yes, but he wouldn't let me have them. I tried to persuade him. I offered an extravagant sum. He was stubborn, he didn't like me, and he was bitterly disappointed in the boy, who turned out a blithering fool."

Accounting probably, Fox thought, for Arthur Tingley's strong feelings on the subject of unmarried mothers. He remarked, "So you made efforts to get the records by—uh—other methods."

"No. I didn't." A corner of Judd's mouth twisted faintly up. "You can't work me into a melodrama. I don't fit. Not even a murder. I knew Arthur's character and had no fear of any molestation during his lifetime, and he conceded me a point. He put the papers in a locked box in his safe and willed the box and its contents to me. Not that he told me where they were. I found that out later."

"When?"

"Three days ago."

Fox's brows went up. "Three *days?*"

"Yes. Monday morning Philip called at my office. I had never seen him since he was a month old, but he established his identity, and he had copies with him of those records. He demanded a million dollars as a donation to some imbecile thing he called Womon. He had it all figured out; it wasn't to be paid to him personally; that was to avoid the income tax. A blackmailer evading the income tax!"

"What was the screw, a threat to publish?"

"Oh, no. He's a blackguard, but he's not a fool. He said that he came to me only because his adopted father would allow him nothing but a pittance—he said pittance—and had practically disinherited him in his will, and he wanted money for this Womon thing. Arthur had been fool enough to let him read the will, and the bequest of the locked box to me had made him smell a rat. As I say, he's not a fool. He had stolen the box from the safe and busted it open, and there it was. His threat was not to publish, but to sue me and my sister for damages, for abandoning him as an infant.

Which of course amounted to the same thing, but that put a face on it. And was something we could not allow to happen under any circumstances, and he knew it."

Fox nodded, with no great display of sympathy. "So why didn't you pay him?"

"Because it was—outrageous. You don't just scribble a voucher for a teller to hand out a million dollars."

"I don't, but you could."

"I didn't. More, because I wanted a guaranty that that would end it. For one thing, I had to be sure I was getting all the original records, and Arthur was the only one who could satisfy me on that, and he wouldn't see me Monday. When I intimated to him on the phone what I wanted to see him about, as plainly as I dared, he took it into his head that I was only using that as an excuse to get at him, in an effort to buy his business, and the stubborn ass refused to see me. I put Philip off for a day by giving him ten thousand dollars. The next morning Arthur phoned me that the box was gone from the safe, but even then he wouldn't come to my office or meet me somewhere, so I had to go to him."

Fox nodded. "Tuesday morning. Name of Brown. I saw you."

"I know you did. But for that mischance—" Judd's quick frown was at himself, at the feeble futility of bewailing a piece of bad luck. "I went to his office, and told him of Philip's demand and threat. He was enraged. His attitude was stupid and dangerous on account of his misconception of Philip's character. He thought Philip could be browbeaten, and I didn't. But what I proposed—I couldn't do anything with him. He would have it his way. It was left that he would talk with Philip at five o'clock that afternoon, and the three of us would have it out the next morning, Wednesday, in his office. I had to accept—"

"That won't do." Fox was shaking his head. "Positively not. Don't try to bounce me off now."

"I'm not trying anything. I am telling you, under coercion—"

"A lie, Mr. Judd. It's no good. You were to meet at Tingley's office Tuesday evening, not Wednesday morning. And you went there. It's too bad that the door you want to keep shut happens to be one I must go through in order to get a murderer, but it does, and you're going to open it. And frankly, the time's getting short. I keep dangling Inspector Damon over you as a threat, but the fact is he's dangling over me too, and—"

There was a knock at the door. They looked that way, and Judd said come in. The door opened and the man in uniform entered.

Judd snapped, "What is it?"

"A gentleman, sir—" The man was approaching with a salver in his hand.

"I'm busy. I'm not here. For anyone."

"Yes, sir. But he insists—"

"Who is it? Here—bring it here!"

The salver was there, and Judd took the card and frowned at it. His eyes narrowed, bored holes in the card, and then lifted to Fox as he extended the card in his hand. Fox took it and saw what it said:

JOSEPH DAMON
Inspector
New York Police Department

Fox met the ominous gleam of suspicion and accu-
sation in the narrowed eyes and spoke to it:

"No."

"If you're playing—"

"I said no." Fox returned the card. "Why don't we
have him in? After all, I only came to inquire about
the offer Consolidated Cereals was making to buy out
the business. Perhaps." He smiled.

"I would prefer—you can wait in another room—"

The two pairs of eyes met, clashed, and decided
the issue. Judd curtly told the man to bring the caller
up, and the man went.

"Probably," Fox speculated, "they've discovered
somehow that you were the mysterious Mr. Brown of
Tuesday morning. They're thorough as the devil on
that kind of thing. Your handling of that is of course
your own business, but if I may offer a little advice,
don't repeat in Damon's presence your suggestion
about my waiting in another room. It might be embarrassing, because I don't intend to."

Guthrie Judd, gently and rhythmically rubbing the
tips of his fingers against each other, made no reply,
and no other movement or sound until he turned his
head at the opening of the door, and arose to greet the
visitor.

Inspector Damon crossed the room and, when he
saw that a hand was going to be offered, shifted a
leather bag he was carrying from his right to his left,
to be able to accept the courtesy. Fox, also on his feet,
was inwardly amused as well as impressed by the
complete lack of surprise or curiosity resulting from
his own, surely unexpected, presence. When his turn
came he extended a hand.

"Good evening, Inspector."

"Hello, Fox. How are you?" There was not even

conventional cordiality in Damon's voice, and his eyes were not even more morose than usual. He turned back: "I'm sorry to have to break in on you, Mr. Judd."

"Quite all right," said Judd crisply. "Sit down. What can I do for you?"

"Why—" Damon shot a glance at Fox. "I'm afraid I have to discuss a very confidential matter with you. If you want to finish your business with Mr. Fox first, I can wait—"

"No no. A confidential matter? Go ahead. I've found—that Fox's discretion can be trusted. Go right ahead."

"I would much prefer," Damon insisted, "to discuss it with you privately."

"But I wouldn't," said Judd sharply. He sat down. "Please get it over with, Inspector. You were admitted, at a moment when I am fairly busy, as a courtesy due your position. Please tell me what you want."

"I assure you, Mr. Judd, you may regret—"

"I never regret anything."

Damon gave it up, sat down and placed a leather bag on the floor in front of him, and hunched over and released the catches and opened it. He straightened up to look at Judd:

"A parcel post package addressed to me by name was delivered at police headquarters at five o'clock this afternoon. It was mailed at 34th Street this morning. Wrapped in brown paper, tied with string, address handprinted with a lead pencil." He bent and got an object from the bag and rested it on his knees. "This was in it. May I ask, have you ever seen it before?"

Judd said, "No."

Damon's eyes moved. "Since you're here, Fox. Have you?"

Fox shook his head. "Not guilty."

"As you see," said Damon, "It's a metal box with a lock, the kind sold by stores as a bond box, best quality, heavy, pretty good lock. Here on the top the letters 'GJ' have been roughly engraved, probably with the point of a knife. The first thing about it is this: a box of this description, including the 'GJ' on its top, was left to you by Arthur Tingley in his will. The police commissioner asked you about it this morning, and you stated you knew nothing of such a box and had no idea what it might contain. You remember that, Mr. Judd?"

"I do," Judd acknowledged. "Hombert told me the will said the box would be found in the safe in Tingley's office, and it wasn't there."

"That's right. The second thing is, the lock has been forced. It was like that when the package was opened. The third thing is the contents." The inspector regarded Judd. "Do you wish to trust them also to Fox's discretion?"

"How do I know? I—go ahead."

"Very well." Damon opened the lid. "Item one, a pair of shoes." He held them up for inspection, and nothing could have been more incongruous in that room and atmosphere as the focus for those stares. They had been worn by a small child, and well worn, so that their surfaces were scuffed, their toes curled up, their soles thin and frayed.

Damon put them on the rug by a leg of his chair. "Item two, a printed folder of the Metropolitan Trust Company, with a list of its officers and a statement of its condition as of June 30, 1939. A circle has been made, with a pen and ink, around the name of Guthrie Judd, President, and a similar circle around the sum of the total resources, six hundred thirty million dollars and something."

He returned the folder to the box and produced the next exhibit. "Item three, a large Manila envelope. It was sealed, but the wax has been broken and the flap slit open. On the outside, in Arthur Tingley's handwriting, is this inscription: 'Confidential. In case of my decease, to be delivered intact to Guthrie Judd. Arthur Tingley. July 9, 1936.'"

Judd had a hand extended. "Then it's mine." His tone was sharp and peremptory. "And you opened it—"

"No, sir, I didn't." Damon showed no indication to turn loose the envelope. "It had already been opened. It is unquestionably your property, and eventually it will be handed over to you, but we shall keep it for the present. Under the circumstances. It contains the birth certificate of 'Baby Philip,' dated September 18, 1911, four pages from the records of the Ellen James Home regarding the sojourn in that institution of a young woman named Martha Judd, and a written statement, holograph, dated July 9, 1936, signed by Arthur Tingley. Also a certificate of the legal adoption of Philip Tingley by Arthur Tingley, dated May 11, 1915. If you wish to inspect these documents, now, in my presence—"

"No," Judd snapped. "I demand the immediate surrender of the box and its contents to me."

Damon regarded him sourly. "For the present, sir—"

"I'll replevy."

"I doubt if you can. Evidence in a murder case—"

"That has nothing to do with Tingley's murder."

"I hope it hasn't." Damon sounded as if he meant it. "You can imagine how much I relished coming here. A man like you and a thing like this. I'm only a cop and you know what you are. I tell you frankly the district attorney should have handled it, and he got from under and wished it onto me. So it's a job, and that's that. You have a sister named Martha. Was she at the Ellen James Home in the year 1911?"

Guthrie Judd folded his arms. "It would have been sensible of you," he said icily, "to follow the district attorney's example. You'll hear from a lawyer in the morning." He aimed a finger at the box. "I advise you to leave that here. It's mine."

"Then you decline to answer any questions about it?"

"I decline to answer any questions about anything. I shall telephone Hombert as soon as you're out of here."

Damon grunted. Methodically, without haste, he returned the papers to the envelope and the envelope to the box, put the shoes on top, closed the lid, replaced the box in the leather bag, snapped the fastenings, and stood up.

"What people like you get away with," he said resentfully. "Here's a story that you know damn well would rate an eight-column spread if it ever got loose, and you act like this and still expect us to keep the cork in. And the hell of it is, we will, and you know it. We've got to." He spun on his heel. "You, Fox, I want to see you. Maybe you're going to phone the commissioner too?"

"I am not," declared Fox, also on his feet. "I'm going along to carry your bag—Have you got anything to say to me, Mr. Judd?"

Judd didn't even look at him. "Look out for the fire," Fox said, and crossed to the door and opened it and went out with the inspector. Together they descended the broad stair, got their coats and hats in the reception hall, and had the door opened for them to the vestibule.

A police car with a uniformed sergeant at the wheel was there at the curb.

"You can come with me," Damon said gruffly, opening the door.

"I intend to." Fox climbed in and slid to the corner. "But we'll go farther and faster if you'll tell him to stop at 914 East 29th."

Damon, sitting down, darted a glance at him. "No. I stopped there on my way uptown, and he's not there. I left a man in front and I'll be notified—"

"I don't like to contradict you, but I'm telling you. Stop at that address and I'll show you something."

"You may," said Damon grimly, "show me several somethings before the night's ended."

"All right, but let's begin with that."

Damon leaned forward and spoke to the driver, and the driver nodded respectfully. The car swung into Park Avenue and sped downtown.

"You might as well be telling me now," said Damon, "how you got on to Judd and go on from there."

"Nope. Not yet. Don't start pushing."

"Did you send me that box?"

"Good God, no. If I had got my hands on that box—"

It had started to rain, a sneaking chilly drizzle, and Fox cranked the window shut on his side. His toe was touching the leather bag which contained the box, and his mind was dancing around the box itself, or rather, around the question, who could conceivably have sent it to the police? It was absolutely weird and completely unaccountable. He progressed beyond that not at all by the time the car rolled to a stop and he jumped out at the heels of the inspector, who warned the sergeant to guard the bag.

A man in a rubber raincoat came from the protection of a near-by doorway and joined them in the vestibule. He responded to the inspector's inquiring glance:

"He hasn't shown up."

"Well," Damon said, "I suppose you'd better—hey! Where the hell did you get that key?"

"Borrowed it." Fox inserted the key and turned it, and opened the door. "Ask me no questions and I'll tell you no lies. We won't need any help."

Damon told the man in the raincoat to stay on post and followed Fox up the dim and dismal stairs. At the top of the four flights he was puffing a little. He watched, inscrutably, saying nothing, at the door in the rear, as Fox tried one of the keys on a ring, abandoned it for another which worked, turned the knob, and swung the door wide. They entered and Fox shut the door.

"I'll take those keys," Damon said. "And if this turns out to be your method of introducing me to another sudden death in the Tingley family—"

He stopped because evidence was before him that his surmise was wrong. Fox had opened the door to the kitchen and they had crowded inside; and the gleam of wrath and hate in the deep-set eyes of the Tingley there on the chair against the water pipe proved that there was plenty of life left in him.

Damon stepped over and took a look at the tape and the knots, and turned to Fox:

"Do you know who did it?"

"Certainly. I did."

"Oh. Nice job. You sure are—" He sighed a little. "I suppose you fixed his jaw, too. Undo him."

Chapter 17

Philip Tingley stood, swaying, clinging to the rim of the gas stove. He tried to open his mouth, grimaced, mumbled something hoarse and unintelligible, and gave it up.

"Here, take a sip of water." Damon proffered a glass. Phil obediently tried it, and swallowed some, went to clear his throat, and winced.

"Bring him inside," Damon said, and led the way to the room at the end of the little hall. Phil followed him, walking none too steadily but prodded on by Fox from the rear. Damon arranged the three chairs so that the light would be full on Phil's face—not, certainly, because it was pleasant to look at—and they sat.

But Damon immediately got up again. "I'm going to get that bag. And have a phone call made." He eyed Fox. "If you try something like taking him down the fire escape and putting him in the furnace—"

He strode out.

Phil's eyes flashed at Fox from beneath their jutting ledges, and he articulated harshly, "You're stronger than I am. I know that." His hands twitched. "If you weren't—"

"Forget it," said Fox unfeelingily. "What do you expect me to do, hold my hands behind my back and let you take three shots? Anyway, you've got a jaw like an alligator."

"She came." There was a quiver under Phil's harshness. "She came, and you—what did you do? Take her to the police?"

"Wait till the inspector comes. He'll be here in a minute."

Phil uttered a sound, half growl and half moan, raised his hand to his swollen jaw, and began a series of cautiously experimental touches and pressures, Fox watching interestedly. That pantomime was still in progress when Damon came tramping in carrying the leather bag, which he deposited on the floor beside his chair.

Fox suggested to him, "If that driver of yours does shorthand—"

"No, thanks," said Damon dryly. "There's enough high explosive in this damn thing to blow me to Staten Island. The district attorney will be here in half an hour, and if he wants to bring in a stenographer he can." He gazed at Phil with unconcealed disfavor. "Fox here says it was him that operated on you and tied you up. Tell me about it."

"If you start it like that," Fox objected, "we'll be here all night. I can give you a brief synopsis—"

"Let's hear it."

"Well," Fox cocked his head, "where'll I start? With a paradox. Philip didn't like the kind of money we have, so he wanted to get hold of a lot of it, to be used for the purpose of proving that it's no good. His foster father, not liking Philip's dislike of money, refused to let him have any, and went so far as to disinherit him, practically, and showed him the will in which he did that. Philip's curiosity was aroused by a bequest to Guthrie Judd of a certain box, and the first time he found himself alone in his father's office with the safe unlocked, he explored and found the box and swiped it. He busted it open and examined the contents—what's the matter?"

Phil was making noises. "That's a lie!" he blurted.

"What's a lie? That you busted it open? Show him the box, Inspector. Why not?"

Damon, after a momentary hesitation, unfastened the bag and produced the box. Phil, gazing at it fascinated, emitted an ejaculation, started up, and was apparently going for it; but it was merely such an involuntary movement as a devoted mother might make at sight of a beloved child restored from danger. He sank back into his chair, still gazing at it.

"We might as well," said Fox, "clean up as we go along. What was the lie?"

"You've got it," Phil mumbled, dazed.

"We sure have. What was the lie?"

"I didn't bust it open."

"No?" Fox stretched to point at the lock. "Look. Metal gouged and twisted. The lock bar wrenched up—"

"I can't help that. I didn't do it. I took it to a locksmith and told him I had lost my key and had him make one that would open it."

"What locksmith? Where?"

"Over on Second Avenue, near 30th. I don't remember the name."

"All right, we'll pass that for the present. Resuming the synopsis. Stop me at lies. Philip discovered his mother's name was Martha Judd, and since the will and the inscription on the envelope both mentioned Guthrie Judd, and it was easy to learn that he had a sister named Martha, that was that. It was also easy to get a folder of the bank of which Judd was president and learn that its resources were over half a billion dollars of no-good money." Fox looked at Phil approvingly. "I like that little touch. Shows a good head for detail."

Damon grumbled, "You were going to be brief."

"I apologize. On Monday, just three days ago, Philip went to see Judd, demanded a million dollars, that being only one six hundred and thirtieth of the total resources, and said if he didn't get it he would sue him and his sister for damages, they having deserted him in infancy. Judd stalled him by giving him ten thousand cash, and squawked to Arthur Tingley. He went to Tingley's office at ten o'clock Tuesday morning—"

"No," Damon put in. "That man's name was Brown."

"For that occasion. It was Judd. Tingley was furious at his adopted son and agreed to help squash him. It was arranged that the three of them should meet at 7:30 that evening in Tingley's office and have it out. At five o'clock—"

"You told me to stop you for lies." Phil's tone was surly. "We were to meet Wednesday morning."

Fox shook his head. "That's washed up. The inspector and I have just had a talk with Judd. That's where I went with—Miss Martha Judd. At five Tuesday afternoon Tingley had a session with Philip and told him to be there at 7:30. But he thought he might need help, so he phoned Amy Duncan, his niece, and asked her to come at seven. So much for Tuesday. Between then and now I have been floundering in a swamp, and still am. But this evening I had a break. I came here to pry something loose from Philip, and

had just finished preparing him for prying, when Miss
Judd arrived and asked me if I was Philip Tingley and
I told her yes. We had an informative talk, and I suggested that we go together to discuss it with Judd. He
resented her taking me for Philip and shooed her upstairs, and he and I were still at it when you arrived."

"Some day," said Damon as if he meant it, "I hope
you sink in a swamp and stay sunk. What I want—"

"Excuse me," said Fox quickly. "Milk me dry before you sell me to the butcher. Remember all I've got
out of Philip so far is growls and dirty looks. Remind
me some time to tell you what happened when I took
him to Judd's office this afternoon. I don't mind it so
much now. Tuesday evening, Judd arrived at the
Tingley building at 7:30, went inside, and came out in
five minutes. Philip arrived at 7:40, went in, and
stayed eight minutes. I suggest that Philip had better
tell us what he saw and did in there, and I can com-
pare it with what Judd told me."

Damon grunted. Phil said sneeringly:

"That's a good trick."

"No, my boy." Fox surveyed him. "Even if you
killed Tingley, the time has come to leave that hole
and try another one. If you didn't kill him, the truth
will do fine. If you did, make up something. After
what Judd told me, the spot you're on is so hot you're
sizzling. He doesn't like you, you know. Is it true that
you went there and found that Tingley and Judd had
decided not to deal with you, to prosecute you for
blackmail? Did you lose your temper and pick up that
weight and crack him on the head, and then—"

"No! I didn't!"

"And then decide you'd better finish it, and go for
a knife—"

"No! The filthy liar! He did it! Judd did it! He was dead when I got there—lying there dead—"

"He was? Was Amy Duncan there too?"

"Yes! On the floor unconscious—not far from him—and Judd had just been there—I didn't know that then but I knew he was going to be there—and I know now—"

Phil was trembling all over. Fox's eyes probed at him, tried to appraise him; for if it was true that Arthur Tingley had been dead at 7:40, he could not very well have been talking on the telephone at eight o'clock.

"Calm down a little," Fox said. "If you're guilty you ought to manage a better show, and if you're innocent you ought to be ashamed of yourself. Did you see anyone else anywhere in the building?"

"No." Phil was trying to stop his trembling.

"Hear anyone or anything?"

"No. It was—very quiet."

"Where did you go besides Tingley's office?"

"Nowhere. I went straight there and straight out."

"You were in there eight minutes. What did you do?"

"I—I felt Amy's pulse. I wanted to get her—out of there—but I didn't dare—and she was breathing all right and her pulse was pretty good. Then I—" Phil stopped.

"Yes? You what?"

"I looked for the box. The safe door was standing open, but it wasn't in there. I looked a few other places, and then I heard Amy move, or thought I did, and I left. Anyway, I thought Judd had been there and killed him and taken the box, so I didn't hope to find it. So I left."

"One thing sure," Damon muttered pessimistically, "you're either a murderer or the best damn specimen of a coward I've ever run across."

But Fox's intent frown did not come from moral condemnation. "Are you aware," he demanded of Phil, "of what you're saying? You had previously stolen the box from the safe and had it in your possession. How the devil could you have been looking for it?"

"I didn't have it in my possession."

"Oh, come. Don't be ass enough—"

"I had had it. I didn't have it then. He came here and found it and took it."

"Who did? When?"

"My father. I mean my brother." Phil laughed shortly and bitterly. "He told me that Tuesday afternoon, that Thomas Tingley was my father. His father. That makes me half Tingley and half Judd, so I ought to be good. He had the box here in the safe, he showed it to me. He had come here that day, I don't know how he got in, and found it and took it."

Fox's frown had deepened. "Are you telling me that at five o'clock Tuesday afternoon—at 5:40, when you left—that box was in Tingley's safe in his office?"

"I am."

"And two hours later, when you returned at 7:40 and found him dead, the box was gone?"

"It was."

"By God," said Damon in utter disgust. "If this is true, it was Guthrie Judd and it's absolutely hopeless. I'm going to have to spend the night with this bony hero—There's Skinner." He got up and started for the front, muttering, "If he didn't like it before, how will he like it now?"

He returned a moment later, bringing with him a thinnish man in a dinner jacket with a skeptical mouth and darting impatient eyes. Fox was on his feet.

"Tecumseh Fox," said Damon, not graciously. "He plays with firecrackers—"

"I know him," said Skinner irritably.

"So you do. Philip Tingley. This is the district attorney—hey, what's the idea?"

"I've got an errand," Fox declared, getting his other arm into his coat sleeve. "I'll be back—"

"No no." Damon snorted scornfully. "You'll stay right here."

Fox put on his hat and looked the inspector in the eye. "Okay," he acquiesced calmly, "if you say so, naturally I stay. But in spite of that synopsis I just gave you, I still know five or six things you don't know. I've got an important errand to do and I'll come back. If you think you and the district attorney can't get along without me for half an hour or so—"

Damon met his gaze, hesitated, and finally nodded. "If this is another of your—"

Fox, not waiting for the rest, turned on his heel and was gone. The door to the hall was open. He left it that way, descended the four flights of stairs, dashed across the sidewalk through the rain to his car, and was pulling the door to when its swing was stopped by the man in the raincoat who had jumped for it.

"Where you going, buddy?"

"Go up and ask the inspector. If he won't tell you, report him. Shut the door, please."

"You don't need to be so damn witty—"

But Fox, having got the engine started and the gear in, didn't wait for that either. The car slid away, gathered speed, and shot off to the west. The clock on the dash said a quarter past eleven. At that hour of the night and in that part of town, despite the rain, it took only a few minutes to make Seventh Avenue and twenty blocks south and around a couple of corners to

320 Grove Street. The pavement there was deserted. Fox stopped directly in front, hopped out and dived through the rain for the vestibule, and, since Olson the watchdog was not at his post, pushed the button above the name "Duncan."

There was no answering click. He tried it again, and then again, with silent intervals between, the third time making it an insistent and importunate series, meanwhile muttering inelegant but expressive imprecations. He was just ready to make a dash through the downpour for a lunchroom at the corner, in search of a phone booth, when a woman came backing into the vestibule from outside—backing in, because she was collapsing an umbrella to get it through the door. That accomplished, she turned, and with a start of surprise saw Fox.

"Lucky again," he observed. "I came for a brief chat with you. No escort at this time of night?"

Amy Duncan's eyes were without sparkle and her skin without bloom. "I went to bed," she said, "and couldn't sleep. So I got up and dressed and went for a walk." She got a key from her bag.

"Didn't Mr. Cliff stick around awhile?"

"No. He went soon after you did. As soon as he had made a few—remarks." She had the door open. "After you—after what you—but I asked you to help me and I suppose I have no right to resent anything. Are you coming up?"

"If I may. I'd like to ask you a couple of questions."

She made no reply, and Fox followed her in and up the stairs. Another key opened the door, and they were in the living room. She turned on the lights.

"Excuse me while I deposit this," she said with dreary politeness, and with the dripping umbrella in her hand crossed and opened another door. Fox, with a sudden unaccountable frown creasing his forehead, stepped forward to get the room she was entering within his range of vision. It was the bathroom, and she was standing the umbrella in the tub to drain. That done, she came out and unbuttoned her coat.

"Blister my belly!" Fox said.

At his tone, she jerked her head up to look at him, and, seeing his face, she goggled. "What—what's the matter?"

"Excuse me," said Fox. "I apologize. I have just been struck by lightning. Rain usually follows lightning, but in this case it preceded it. I no longer need to ask you any questions. You are a beautiful and enchanting creature, and whereas I loved you before I now adore you. Good night and happy dreams."

She was still goggling when the door had closed behind his exit.

Fox did not descend the stairs rapidly. He went down, and out to his car, slowly and deliberately, like a man whose head is so completely engrossed with other matters that his feet, in their wisdom, are quite aware that the detail of locomotion is being left to them with no assistance from above. In the car behind the wheel, he sat a long time without moving, staring at the globules dancing down the windshield with a concentration that could not have been surpassed by his eighteenth century namesake, the statesman Charles James Fox, when he wagered fifty thousand pounds with Richard Brinsley Sheridan on a raindrop race down a club window. Finally, still deliberately, he turned the ignition key; and it took him twice as long to retrace the route to 914 East 29th Street as it had taken him to come.

He exchanged nods with the man in the raincoat, who seemed relieved to see him back, pressed the button and opened the door on the click, and mounted the four flights for the fourth time that day. The door above was open, and Inspector Damon, standing there, rumbled at sight of him:

"It's about time. Come on in here. The D.A. wants to hear—"

"Let him wait." Fox, no longer deliberate, was crisp. He pushed by and entered the kitchen. "The place for a D.A. is a courtroom. Come in here instead, and shut the door. I've got it."

Damon, being fairly well acquainted with Fox's tones of voice and manners of speech, after one sharp glance at him, stepped inside the kitchen and quietly closed the door.

"All right," he said, "I'll bite. What have you got?"

"I *think* I have," Fox amended. "Do me a favor. Bring that box here."

The inspector regarded him. "I don't know. I'm aware that you pick up a lot of gossip, but—"

"Now come. Just bring it here, huh?"

Damon went, and in a moment he was back with the leather bag. He placed it on the table and removed the box and handed it to Fox. Then he stood in readiness to take appropriate action in the remote event that Fox had gone crazy.

It did in fact appear that Fox's mind was touched, though not in a way that justified restraint by force, for instead of opening the box, he grasped it firmly in both hands and shook it violently from side to side. His attitude suggested that he was listening for something, but the banging of the shoes against the metal sides of the box was all there was to hear. He stopped and gazed at the box a moment with his lips screwed up, waggled it again as before but more gently, returned it to the bag, and looked at the inspector with a nod of satisfaction.

"That's all right," he declared. "I've got it. I know who killed Tingley."

"That's fine," said Damon sarcastically. "That's just fine. Name and address?"

Fox shook his head. "Not yet. And for God's sake don't start shoving, because it'll only lead to an argument and you can't win it."

"I can if—"

"No, you can't. You've got nothing to open me with because you haven't the faintest idea where the joker is. You admitted in there that as far as you can see it's Guthrie Judd and it's hopeless. I'm not sticking out my tongue at you, I'm just stating a fact. If you'll just tell me one or two things—for instance, were there any prints on the box?"

"Ha, by God. I'm to tell you."

Fox upturned his palms. "Be reasonable. Will it stop your circulation to tell me if there were prints on the box?"

"No. There weren't any. It had been wiped."

"Any on the stuff inside?"

"Yes. Plenty. Tingley's and Philip's and a mess of old ones."

"Much obliged. That fits. Have you still got a man in Tingley's office?"

"I've got two men. Six men on three shifts. We couldn't seal the room because they needed things."

"Fine. Have you removed anything from the room?"

"Certainly we have."

"What?"

Damon shifted, went closer, so that his eyes, straight into Fox's, were only inches away. "You know," he said in a hard tone, "if there is any chance, any chance at all, that this is a ride around the block—"

"There isn't. I have more sense. What was taken from the room?"

"The corpse. Two bloody towels. The knife and the weight and Miss Duncan's bag. Five small jars with some stuff in them which we found in a drawer of Tingley's desk. We had the stuff analyzed for quinine and there wasn't any. We were told they were just routine samples."

"That's all?"

"Yes."

"No other sample jars were found?"

"No. I didn't do the searching myself, but those five were brought to me, and if any others had been there they would have been brought too."

"Then it's still there. It ought to be. It must be. Get your hat and coat and let's go see."

Damon, showing no inclination to move, demanded, "What and where?"

"I'll show you. Tingley's office. I swear by heaven, if you balk on me I'll spill it to the D.A. and get him to go with me, and leave you to chew the rag with that bony wonder in there. Well?"

Damon, scowling, said, "You wait here," picked up the leather bag, and stalked off in the direction of the inner room. Fox heard him speaking with Skinner, and then he reappeared and gestured to Fox to go ahead, and they left the apartment. Downstairs in the vestibule the man in the raincoat was instructed to go up and stay with the district attorney, and he went. There ensued a brief argument about cars, which Fox won: he would drive his own, and the inspector would follow in the police car.

To the old Tingley landmark on 26th Street it was even a shorter distance than it had been to 320 Grove Street, and within a few minutes the cars came to a stop again at the curb, nose to tail, and the two men joined company again at the stone steps and entered together, Damon opening the door with a key. Inside it was pitch-dark. The inspector produced a flashlight, and with the aid of its beam they mounted the stairs and threaded their way through the maze of doors and partitions, not bothering to turn on any lights. When they got to the door bearing the ancient legend, THOMAS TINGLEY, they found it wide open, and a large man with a slight strabismus in his left eye was standing just outside with an automatic in his hand. At sight of them he looked simultaneously relieved and disappointed.

"Hello, Drucker."

"Good evening, Inspector." The man moved aside to let them enter.

The table and chairs which had been in the middle of the room for the afternoon meeting of the trustees were no longer there; the table was now at the far end near a window, littered with newspapers and a deck of playing cards, and standing beside it, just up from a chair, was a man with a thin little mouth in a big face.

Damon tossed him a nod. "Hello, Bowen." His head pivoted slowly, to the right and then to the left, taking in everything. He ended with Drucker, who had followed them in. "Nothing to report?"

"No, sir. Nothing but monotony."

Damon transferred to Fox. "Well? Show me."

Fox walked to the safe and grasped the lever of the door, but it wouldn't budge.

"They keep things in there," said Drucker.

"Checks and things. They open it in the morning and close it in the afternoon."

Fox frowned. "That sounds pretty loose to me."

"Stalling?" The inspector snorted. "I told you why we didn't seal it. Everything that goes out, and everything that comes in, is handled and checked. Perhaps you'd like to prepare a new set of regulations?"

"No, thanks, Inspector. Don't bristle. Cooperate. If you have the combination of the safe—"

"I haven't. But I say you're stalling. That safe was searched by Lieutenant Rowcliff Tuesday night, and he never yet let a cubic millimeter get by."

"Did Rowcliff do this room?"

"He did. With assistance."

"Mmm." Fox shook his head and bit his lower lip. "Then the safe's out. So is the desk, and everything else that can be ruled and calipered." He slowly surveyed the room, the shelves and cabinets, the photographs on the walls, the piles of trade journals, the desk, Tingley's coat on its hanger and the hat on the little shelf above, the screen and wash basin.

"It looks like a job," he admitted. "I'm not stalling. I think it's here. I hope to heaven it's here. But it looks like an all-night job. There is, of course, one chance. A squad of scientific searchers might possibly be too scientific. I mean they might overlook something so obvious that science would sneer at it." He glanced around. "For instance, take that hat there on the shelf. What if Tingley simply stuck it under his hat?" He crossed the room and reached up for the hat. "Not that I'm expecting—"

He stopped short, with his voice, but not with his hand.

The next thirty seconds were comic relief. When Damon and Drucker saw, as they did, that an object on the shelf had been concealed under the hat and that Fox was grabbing it, they made for him. Fox, seizing it, held it in the air out of their reach, and they attacked him, jumped for it, pulled at him. It was like a boy protecting an apple against the raid of hungry and covetous pals.

"Prints, you damned fool!" Drucker screamed.

"Let go! Cut it out!" Fox shook them off and back-stepped away. "To hell with prints! I'm not interested in prints." They stood and glared at him as he raised the object—a little glass jar with no cover—to his nose and sniffed at it. "I'm interested in something else. Who found it, anyhow? Let me alone." He got a penknife from his pocket and opened a blade, with its tip dug out a little of the stuff in the jar, and conveyed it to his mouth. While his lips and cheeks moved to facilitate dissolution in that primitive laboratory re-tort, the others watched in silent fascination.

"Brrr," he said, and made a horrible face, holding the jar out to Damon. "Grand for a febrifuge. Have a little."

The inspector took the jar. "And you knew it was under the hat," he said grimly. "And you either put it there yourself Tuesday night, expecting us to find it, or you—"

"You're a tadpole," said Fox, loud enough to stop him. "You make me sick, and if you'll send your subor-dinates from the room I'll tell you what else you make me. Also it's midnight and I'm going home. It takes me over an hour to get there, and during that time I'll be trying to tidy up the inside of my head. I'll be back here at ten in the morning, and I respectfully request you to meet me here with the box, the jar, Miss Duncan, Mr. Cliff, Philip, and Guthrie Judd. If you want me to bring Judd, phone me before I leave home, which will be at 8:40. I presume that Miss Murphy and Miss Yates and Mr. Fry will be on the premises. I did not know that the jar was under the hat, and it was a moment I shall never forget."

Chapter 18

Amy Duncan sat on a wooden straight-backed chair, with her eyes downcast, her hands tightly clasped in her lap, and a weary tenseness in every muscle of her body. It was the first time she had been in that room since, sixty-two hours before, she had regained consciousness there on the floor and opened her eyes on the most hideous sight she had ever seen. She had had to control a shudder of repugnance when she had entered some minutes previously; now she sat numbly waiting for whatever was going to be done. Without having to move her eyes, she looked at her wrist watch; it was ten after ten. It was bright and sunny outside, and when she raised her heavy lids the glare from the windows, which she as well as others was facing, made her blink with discomfort.

There was no one there she cared to talk to, even if conversation had been in order, which it apparently wasn't. There were seven other persons in the room, and several empty chairs, brought in for the occasion. Not far from her on the left was a man she didn't know—a man more than twice her age, well-dressed, erect on his chair, his mouth tight in the control of acerbity. She had heard him addressed as Mr. Judd. Beyond him was Leonard Cliff, and beyond Cliff was her cousin Philip. Toward the windows a man was seated at a table with a notebook open in front of him, and standing behind him was Inspector Damon. On the table was a leather bag. Another man was seated in the rear, near the door, and still another was standing by the safe, which was at her right. No one was saying anything.

The door which led to the factory opened, and Carrie Murphy entered. Amy nodded at her and she nodded back. She was followed by Mr. Fry, Miss Yates, and Tecumseh Fox. While Fox crossed to join Inspector Damon, the other three sought empty chairs and occupied them.

Fox muttered to Damon, "Okay."

Damon morosely surveyed the faces before him and said loudly, "This is an official inquiry." It came out hoarse, and he cleared his throat. "I announce that because Mr. Fox is going to say some things and ask some questions, and he is not connected with the police, but that's our business and not yours. Everything said here will be taken down and will be a part of the official record. Mr. Guthrie Judd asked permission to have a lawyer present and it was refused. He is completely at liberty to say nothing or to say anything he wants to, and that is true of all of you." He shot a glance at the man with the notebook. "Got that, Corey?"

"Yes, sir."

"Good," Damon folded his arms. "Go ahead, Fox."

Fox moved to one side of the table, faced the little audience, and spoke in a quiet and even pleasant tone. "I'm going to ask you only about things I already know, and for the most part things you've already told me, so there really shouldn't be much to it. Also, I'll make it brief if you will. Miss Murphy; did you go to Miss Yates's apartment around 7:30 Tuesday evening to discuss something with her?"

Carrie Murphy nodded, and, as Fox waited, said, "Yes," in a low tone.

"Did she call someone on the phone?"

"Yes."

"Whom did she call and at what time?"

"Mr. Arthur Tingley. It was eight o'clock, just a minute or two before."

"At his home or his office?"

"At his office. She tried his home first, but he wasn't there, so she called here and got him."

They were all looking at Carrie, and Philip was staring at her in unconcealed astonishment. Fox went on:

"Did you talk to Tingley yourself? Did you hear his voice?"

"No, but it was him. What she said—it must have been him."

Fox's eyes moved. "Miss Yates. Is Miss Murphy's statement correct?"

"It is," said Miss Yates firmly.

"You recognized Tingley's voice?"

"Certainly. I've been hearing it all my life—"

"Of course you have. Thanks. Mr. Philip Tingley; on Tuesday afternoon did your father—let's just say father, shall we?—did he ask you to come here at 7:30 that evening?"

"Yes!" Phil said, loudly and aggressively.

"For what purpose?"

"To have—to discuss something with him and that man." Phil pointed with a long bony rigid finger. "Guthrie Judd."

"Did you come?"

"Yes, but not at 7:30. I was ten minutes late."

"Did you enter the building and come to this room?"

"Yes! And I saw Arthur Tingley on the floor behind the screen, dead, and I saw Amy Duncan there, too, unconscious, and I felt her pulse and—"

"Of course. Naturally, being human, you displayed humanity. Are you sure Arthur Tingley was dead?"

"I am. If you had seen him—"

"I did see him. His throat had been cut?"

"Yes, and the blood had spread on the floor until it was only a few inches away from Amy's face—"

"Thank you," Fox said curtly, and moved his eyes. "Mr. Leonard Cliff. Did you follow Amy Duncan from her apartment to this building on Tuesday evening?"

Amy's head jerked sidewise. Cliff's remained stationary. He spoke in a muffled tone: "I did, as I told you."

"What time did you arrive?"

"About ten minutes after seven."

"Miss Duncan entered this building?"

"Yes."

"What did you do from then until eleven minutes after eight, when she came out again?"

"I stood in the entrance of the driveway tunnel. It was raining."

"Did you see Philip Tingley arrive at 7:40?"

"I did, and I saw him come out again seven or eight minutes later."

"Did you see anyone else arrive?"

"Yes, before that. At 7:30 a limousine drove up and stopped directly in front, and a man got out and crossed the sidewalk to the entrance with the driver holding an umbrella over him."

"Wait a minute!" Inspector Damon said peremptorily, stepping forward. His eyes met Fox's. "We'll stop this right here." He faced Cliff and snapped at him. "Did you enter the building?"

"No."

"What were you doing here? Why did you follow Miss Duncan?"

Cliff's mouth opened and shut. He looked appealingly at Fox.

Fox plucked at Damon's sleeve. "Inspector, please. This is on the record, you know, and we don't need that detail. Take my word for it. Or get it later. It'll keep—Mr. Cliff, what was the registration number on the limousine?"

"GJ55."

"And who was the man who got out and entered this building?"

"To the best of my belief, it was Guthrie Judd. It was dark and rainy and I wasn't able—"

"We understand that. How long did he stay in the building?"

"Five minutes. Between four and six minutes."

"He came out and got in the limousine and it drove off?"

"Yes."

Fox nodded, and shifted his gaze. "Mr. Guthrie Judd."

The two pairs of eyes met in mid-air like gamecocks leaping for the thrust of battle, but then Fox smiled at him.

"Well, sir," Fox said, "it looks as if we need you for a referee. Miss Yates says Tingley was alive at eight o'clock, and Philip says he was dead at 7:40. We'd like to hear from you what shape he was in at 7:30. You were inside the building five minutes. You can of course say that you didn't come upstairs, or that you came to this room and found it empty, but we wouldn't believe you, and neither would a judge or jury. What may be more to the point in your case, nor would ten million newspaper readers."

There was movement in the muscles of Judd's jaw.

"You realize," Fox went on, "that I am not bound, as the law officers are, to protect the embarrassing secrets of prominent people from the public curiosity. And probably newspaper readers would be even more interested in the contents of that box with GJ on it than in your brief visit here Tuesday evening. Not only the story itself, which is full of human interest, but those shoes! A pair of baby shoes—"

"He was dead," said Judd, biting the words off.

"Ah! Then you did come up to this room?"

"Yes. He was on the floor with his throat cut. Near him was a young woman I had never seen, unconscious. I was in the room less than a minute. I had come through all the doors to this room with some hesitation, because I had heard no sound and had stopped in the anteroom to call Tingley's name, and had got no response. I returned—cautiously. Under the circumstances."

Fox nodded. "I suppose that could have taken five minutes. I am not a policeman, and I'm certainly not the district attorney, but I think it is quite likely that you will never be under the necessity of telling this story in a courtroom. They won't want to inconvenience you. However, in the event that a subpoena takes you to the witness stand, are you prepared to swear to the truth of what you have just said?"

"I am."

"Thank you very much." Fox's gaze swept an arc to include the others. "You see what we're up against.

According to Miss Yates, Tingley was alive at eight o'clock, and according to Philip and Judd, he couldn't have been." His gaze suddenly fixed. "Are you still positive it was Tingley you talked to, Miss Yates?"

She met his eyes squarely. "I am." Her voice was perfectly controlled. "I don't say they're lying. I don't know. I only know if it was someone imitating Arthur Tingley's voice, I've never heard anything to equal it."

"You still think it was him."

"I do."

"Why did you tell me—on Wednesday, there in the sauce room—why did you tell me that when you got home Tuesday evening you stood your umbrella in the bathtub to drain?"

"Because I—"

She stopped, and it was easy to tell from her face what happened. An alarm had sounded. Some nerve band had carried the lightning message: "Look out!" Any eye might have seen it, and to a trained eye it was so patent that Inspector Damon emitted a little growl and involuntarily straightened his shoulders. All were looking at her.

"Why," she asked, her soprano voice a shade thinner than it had been, but quite composed, "did I say that? I don't remember it."

"I do," Fox declared. "The reason I bring it up, you also told me you left here at a quarter past six and went straight home, which is only a five-minute walk. It didn't start raining that evening until three minutes to seven, so I wondered why your umbrella needed draining at 6:20."

"Then why didn't you ask me?"

"A darned good question," Fox conceded. "First, ignorance. At that time I didn't know when the rain had started. Second, poverty of intellect. When I found out, accidentally, what time the rain started, I couldn't remember why it should have started earlier."

"But you remember it now? That I said that? I don't."

"Well, I do." Fox wouldn't let her eyes away from him. "There are, of course, two possible explanations. One, that your umbrella got wet without any rain, say from a fire hose. Two, that you left here to go home, not at 6:15 as you said you did, but considerably later. May I tell you why I like the second explanation best?"

Miss Yates snorted. She looked at Damon. "Inspector, you say this is an official inquiry. It sounds to me more like this man showing off and making a poor job of it. What he remembers, what I said to him that I didn't say . . ."

"Don't answer him if you don't want to," Damon said dryly.

"But this is a place of business and I have something better to do—"

"I won't keep you much longer," Fox assured her, "and I have no more questions to ask. I just want to tell you that I like the second explanation best because it fits so well into the only satisfactory theory of the murder of Arthur Tingley. If you had gone home at 6:15, as you said, you couldn't very well have been here to knock Miss Duncan on the head when she arrived at ten minutes past seven. Of course you could have gone and returned here, that's possible though unlikely, and it wouldn't change things any."

Miss Yates said nothing, but she smiled. It was the first time Fox had seen her smile. He shot a glance at Damon, Damon made a quick gesture to the man who stood by the safe, and the man moved to within an arm's length of Miss Yates's chair.

"The theory starts back a few weeks," Fox resumed. "As you remarked to me on Wednesday, this business and this place were everything to you; you had no life except here. When P. and B. made an offer to buy the business you became alarmed, and upon reflection you were convinced that sooner or later Tingley would sell. This old place would of course be abandoned. That was intolerable to you. You considered ways of preventing it, and what you hit on was adulterating the product, damaging its reputation sufficiently so that P. and B. wouldn't want it. You chose what seemed to you the lesser of two evils. Doubtless you thought that the reputation could be gradually reestablished."

Sol Fry, who, like the others, had been dividing his attention, deliberately turned half around in his chair and stared at Miss Yates incredulously. She was unaware of it, for she wasn't looking at him.

"It seemed probable," Fox conceded, "that it would work. The only trouble was, you were overconfident. You were in your own mind so completely identified with the success and very existence of this place and what went on here, that you never dreamed that Tingley would arrange with your subordinates to check on you secretly. Tuesday afternoon you learned about it when Fry caught Miss Murphy in the act. And you had no time to consider the situation, to do anything about it, for almost immediately afterward —at a quarter to six, just after he phoned his niece to come and help him with his adopted son—Tingley called you into his office and accused you."

"You were behind the desk and heard him," said Miss Yates sarcastically.

"No, I wasn't. But I'll finish with the theory. Tingley not only accused you, he told you that he had proof. He had got from Carrie Murphy a jar containing a sample of one of your mixes, and it had quinine in it. Knowing his temper, I suspect that he not only fired you but announced that he was going to prosecute, but that isn't essential to the theory, for I know he told you he was going to sell the business. At least he phoned to Leonard Cliff, undoubtedly in your presence, and made an appointment to see him the next morning, and there could have been only one reason for that. I suppose you implored him, pleaded with him, and were still pleading with him, from behind, while he was stooping over the basin behind the screen to wash his hands. He didn't know you had got the two-pound weight from his desk, and never did know it. It knocked him out. You went and got a knife and finished the job, there where he lay on the floor, and you were searching the room, looking for the sample jar which he had got from Carrie Murphy, when you heard footsteps."

Only the man standing near Miss Yates's chair could see the rhythmic contortions of her fingers in her lap.

"Naturally that alarmed you," Fox continued. "But the steps were of only one person, and that a woman. So you stood behind the screen with the weight in your hand, hoping that whoever it was she would come straight to that room and enter it, and she did. She even obligingly stopped, became motionless, just at the spot where you could hit her without first taking a step. You dragged her behind the screen, as a precaution in the event of the arrival of another unexpected caller, and you got an idea upon which you immediately acted by pressing her fingers around the knife handle, from which of course your own prints had been wiped—"

A stifled gasp interrupted him—from Amy Duncan, who was staring at Miss Yates in horrified disbelief.

Fox answered it without moving his eyes from Miss Yates. "I doubt if you intended to incriminate Miss Duncan. You probably calculated—and for an impromptu and rapid calcuation it was a good one—that when it was found that the weight had been wiped and the knife handle had not, the inference would be, not that Miss Duncan had killed Tingley, but that the murderer had clumsily tried to pin it on her. That tended to divert suspicion from you, for it was known that you had been on friendly terms with her and bore her no grudge. It was a very pretty calculation for a hasty one. Hasty, because now you were in a hurry, and you hadn't found the jar. You were so hasty that when Tingley's coat slipped off its hanger while you were searching the pockets you left it lying on the floor. I suppose you had previously found that the safe door was open and had looked in there, but now you tried it again. No jar was visible, but a locked metal box was there on a shelf, and you picked it up and shook it."

Damon muttered involuntarily, "I'll be damned."

"You shook it," Fox repeated, "and it sounded as if the jar was in it. Not exactly, perhaps, but near enough to you as you were then. You were getting panicky. Amy's arrival had unnerved you. If she could appear unexpectedly, anyone could, a regiment could. The box was locked. To go to the factory again and get something to pry it open with—no. Enough. Besides, the jar was in no other likely place, so that must be it. Your nerves couldn't take any more. You took the box

and went, leaving by the stairs in the rear and the
delivery entrance. You may even have been startled
into a precipitate exit by the sound of more footsteps
on those old stairs, for Guthrie Judd arrived only ten
minutes after Miss Duncan did. You hurried home
through the rain, for it was certainly raining then, and
had just got your umbrella stood in the tub to drain
and your things off when Carrie Murphy arrived."

"But she—she—" Carrie stammered.

"I know, Miss Murphy. She was dry and composed
and herself. An exceptionally cool and competent
head has for thirty years been content to busy itself
with titbits." Fox's gaze was still at Miss Yates.
"While you were talking with Miss Murphy you had
an idea. You would lead the conversation to a point
where a phone call to Tingley would be appropriate,
and you did so; and you called his house first and then
his office, and faked a conversation with him. The idea
itself was fairly clever, but your follow-up was brilliant. You didn't mention it to the police, and advised
Miss Murphy not to, realizing it would backfire if
someone entered this office between the time you left
and eight o'clock. If it turned out that someone had,
and Miss Murphy blabbed about the phone call, you
could say that you had pretended to make it for the
effect on her, and adduce the fact that you hadn't
tried to fool the police about it; if it turned out that
someone hadn't, the phone call would stick, with Miss
Murphy to corroborate it."

A low growl came from Damon.

"Excuse me," Fox said. "But you couldn't open the
box while Miss Murphy was there, and before she left
your friend Miss Harley arrived to play cribbage. You
could of course have said you had a headache and sent
Miss Harley away, but, not knowing when Miss

Duncan would regain consciousness, or even, as a matter of fact, whether she ever would, you wanted an alibi to as late an hour as possible. So you swallowed your anxiety and played cribbage for two and a half hours. As soon as Miss Harley had gone you forced the lid open with something, say a heavy screwdriver—and I can imagine your disappointment and dismay when you saw no jar. Only a pair of child's shoes and an envelope!

"I doubt if you returned here that night. You may have, for you certainly wanted that jar, but I doubt if you had the guts. If you did, naturally you moved with caution, and you either didn't enter this room because you heard me in here, or you did enter it, failed to find the jar, and fled again when you heard the police arriving shortly after midnight. Or perhaps it took you a while to screw your courage up to it, and when you finally did come the police were already here. I know you were at home at ten minutes to twelve, for at that time I phoned to you at your apartment. Those are speculations; in any event, you didn't get the jar."

Fox paused for breath; and Miss Yates snapped at Inspector Damon, "Is this going on all day?"

Damon neither spoke nor moved. Fox continued:

"I'm about done. But you deserve to hear this: your mailing that box to the inspector this morning was extremely stupid. I realize that you didn't want it in your flat, and that your suspense about the jar must have been terrific, since you knew Miss Murphy had told me about the samples secretly delivered to Tingley. But why didn't you fill the box with stones and throw it in the river? Or if stones are scarce at your place, anything with enough weight? I suppose you put on a pair of gloves, examined the contents of the envelope, and figured that if the police got hold of it their attention would be directed to Guthrie Judd and Philip. So you wiped the box clean of prints and wrapped it and mailed it. I hope you see now how dumb that was. Instead of directing suspicion against Philip or Judd, the result was just the opposite, for it was obvious that neither of them would have mailed the box to the police, and therefore some third person had somehow got possession of the box, and the who and how became immediately the most important questions to get answered."

If anyone looked away from Miss Yates at that moment for a glance at Fox, they saw a glint of something resembling admiration in his eyes. "I can see," he said, "that though your brain may have gone fuzzy on you when you decided to mail that box, it is clear and cool now. You know where you stand, don't you? You realize that I can prove little or nothing of what I've said. I can't prove what Tingley said to you Tuesday evening, or what time you left here, or that you got the box from the safe and took it with you, or that it was you who mailed it to the police. I can't even prove that there wasn't someone here at eight o'clock who imitated Tingley's voice and deceived you into thinking that he was talking to you on the phone. I can't actually prove a darned thing. That's what's in your head, and you're right. So I'll have to take back what I said a little while ago, that I had no more questions to ask. I'd like to put one or two to Miss Murphy." Fox turned to reach a hand into the leather bag, and when he withdrew it there was something in it. He stepped forward, circling around Philip's chair, and was standing in front of Carrie Murphy. He held the object in front of her eyes.

"Please look at this carefully, Miss Murphy. As

you see, it is a small jar half full of something. Pasted
on it is a small plain white label bearing the notation
in pencil, 'eleven dash fourteen dash Y.' Does that
mean anything to you? Look at it—"

But Carrie had no chance to give it a thorough
inspection, let alone voice her fatal response. The figure of Miss Yates, from eight feet away, came hurtling
through the air. She uttered no frenzied cry, uttered
no sound at all, but flung herself with such unexpected speed and force that the fingers of her outstretched hand, missing what they were after, nearly
poked Fox's eye out. He grabbed for the wrist and got
it, and then the man who had been on the other side of
her chair was there and had her. He seized her from
behind by her upper arms, with a grip that must have
made her flesh wince, but apparently she didn't feel it.
She stood, with no protest or attempt to struggle,
looked at Tecumseh Fox, who had backed away, and
asked him what Fox afterwards said was the most
startling question—under the circumstances—that
had ever been addressed to him:

"Where was it?"

He told her.

Half an hour later, down on the street, Fox had his
foot on the running board of his car ready to climb in
when he felt a touch at his elbow, turned, and saw it
was Leonard Cliff.

"Beg pardon," Cliff said. His eyes had that peculiar fixed vacancy which eyes have when the object
they are focused on is not the one they are seeing.
Amy Duncan's eyes, from where she sat at the other
end of the driver's seat, were more honestly directed.
She was looking at Cliff.

It appeared that Cliff didn't intend to go on until pardon had been granted, so Fox asked politely, "Want something? Can we give you a lift? We're going down to Grove Street—"

"I'll take a taxi, thank you," Cliff said stiffly. "I wanted to ask if you wouldn't come to my office some day next week and meet the president of the company. I was very much impressed by the way you handled that up there. We are one of the largest corporations in the country, and we could make a very tempting offer—"

"You're a liar," Fox said bluntly. "I mean that isn't what you touched my elbow for, at this particular moment. Your corporation doesn't need me that bad. You simply couldn't resist the desire to get close to Miss Duncan."

"Really," said Cliff. "Really—"

"Yep, really. By the way, I've just told her why you were tailing her Tuesday evening, and she didn't laugh. Far from it."

"Well, that—that is no longer of any . . ." It ran off into nothing, because his eyes had had their way and were meeting Amy's.

"Hop in," Fox invited him. "We're going to stop in at Grove Street for Miss Duncan's umbrella. She's going to give it to me to add to my collection of souvenirs. Go around to the other side and squeeze in with us. Then we're going to Rusterman's for lunch."

"I—I'll get in the back."

"There's plenty of room," said Amy, who up to that point had taken no part in the conversation.

Cliff hesitated, looked like a man who feared he was looking like a fool, and then moved. He went around the front of the car and was at the other door, which Amy had swung open. She moved over against

Fox, but even so it was fairly close quarters. When Cliff got the door closed he was touching her all along the frontier. There was no help for it.

The car rolled east. As it turned into Eighth Avenue Cliff said, "Of course you didn't invite me for lunch, but it would be very—I mean if you would both accept an invitation from me—at Rusterman's if you like it there—"

"Nothing doing," Fox said firmly. "You've been neglecting your business all week and you'd better start catching up. Besides, Miss Duncan and I met romantically and we're going to part romantically. I'll drop you off wherever you say. Your office?"

So Mr. Cliff worked that afternoon—at least, he was at his desk. The evening was another matter. The End.

The World of
Rex Stout

Now, for the first time ever, enjoy a peek into the life of Nero Wolfe's creator, Rex Stout, courtesy of the Stout Estate. Pulled from Rex Stout's own archives, here are rarely seen, some never-before-published memorabilia. Each title in "The Rex Stout Library" will offer an exclusive look into the life of the man who gave Nero Wolfe life.

Bad for Business

One of Rex Stout's great passions (besides the events of a certain brownstone on West 35th Street) was his work with the Author's League of America. Following is a newspaper clipping from 1951 which describes Stout being elected to head that organization.

Mystery Writer Elected
Head of Authors League

Rex Stout

The Authors League of America elected Rex T. Stout, mystery story writer and lecturer, as its president at a membership meeting yesterday in the Barbizon Plaza Hotel. Mr. Stout, who succeeds Oscar Hammerstein 2d, is the creator of the character Nero Wolfe, super-detective. He lives in Brewster, N. Y.

John Hersey, vice president of the league and author of "A Bell for Adano" and "The Wall," presided at the meeting, which was not open to reporters. After the meeting he said that no other officers had been elected because of a pending amendment to the league's constitution providing for two vice presidents.

John Schulman, an attorney for the Authors League, made a report on information he had gathered here and abroad concerning proposed changes in international copyright laws.

Printed in the United States
by Baker & Taylor Publisher Services